How can Loralie convince Denis she is innocent?

"You-you-you—!" Words seemed to fail him. His sparking brown eyes said plenty, though. "You disgust me," he hissed at last.

"What are you talking about?" Loralie felt as though she'd been struck.

"Don't act so innocent," he sneered.

"Denis, please. I have no idea what you're talking about."

"I'll bet you don't, you lying cheat."

Loralie's own anger suddenly escalated. She clenched the fabric of her dress to keep herself from slapping his face.

BRENDA BANCROFT is a pen name of inspirational romance author Susan Feldhake. At home in central Illinois with her husband, Steven, and four children, she is employed as writing instructor for a college-accredited correspondence school. In her spare time she likes to hike, listen to country and western music, and fellowship with close friends.

Books by BRENDA BANCROFT

HEARTSONG PRESENTS

HP22—Indy Girl
HP30—A Love Meant to Be
HP35—When Comes the Dawn

ROMANCE READER—TWO BOOKS IN ONE
(Under the pen name Susan Fledhake)

RR7—For Love Alone & Love's Sweet Promise

Don't miss out on any of our super romances. Write to us at the following address for information on our newest releases and club information.

Heartsong Presents Readers' Service
P.O. Box 719
Uhrichsville, OH 44683

A Real and Precious Thing

Brenda Bancroft

Heartsong Presents

ISBN 1-55748-464-3

A REAL AND PRECIOUS THING

PRINTED IN THE U.S.A.

one

Loralie Morgan leaned forward to see out the plane window. Her bird's-eye view of the spring-colored patchwork quilt below made her glad she had requested a window seat.

"We're approaching Lambert Field in St. Louis." The pilot's voice came over the inter-communications system of the 707 she'd boarded in Atlanta. "We should be arriving at the gate in ten minutes. We hope you enjoyed your flight, and it is our wish that you'll fly with us again. Have a nice day!"

When the pilot clicked off his microphone, Loralie shifted in her seat. A panorama of consider-ations vied for her attention. She hoped there would be a taxi waiting in front of the terminal. She tried not to think of the possibility that her small valise might not have made the same flight to the Gateway City that she had. She also tried to push from her mind the fear that there would be a problem with her hotel reservation. What would she do if she arrived at the hotel and they hadn't any record of her reservation made months earlier? The thought of the hotel was like an anchor in the shifting sea of unknown possibili-ties, for she knew just where the hotel was; a city map of St. Louis had shown her it was within walking distance of the downtown Cervantes Convention Center, just a skip and a hop from the Martin Luther King Bridge that crossed the mighty Mississippi River.

"Your first flight?" asked the retirement-age gentleman in the seat next to her.

Loralie gave him a quick, puzzled smile. "Oh, no. Why. . .?"

He shrugged. "You seem a little nervous."

"Do I?" she countered. Then she gave a light, self-conscious laugh. "I guess I am—but not about flying. I'm in town on business."

"Big meeting?" asked the man. He looked like someone who had once been a business executive, and his tone was understanding.

"Well, in a way, yes."

He nodded as though he knew what she meant. So understanding did he seem, she almost expected him to bring forth a roll of antacids to quell her nervous stomach.

"What business are you in?" he inquired.

"Numismatics."

He nodded, but Loralie wasn't sure he really understood. "I was with AT&T for thirty years. I retired two years ago. The early-out option."

Loralie remembered reading about the trimming of the AT&T work force. It had made news nationwide. But then, almost every big company had faced the same sort of thing, whether through attrition, early-retirement offers, or layoffs.

By comparison, she felt herself fortunate. She wasn't at the mercy of a large, sometimes impersonal corporation. As a self-employed business person, she knew the sky was the limit if she worked hard, invested wisely, and wore the hats of both boss and employee until she could build her business to the point where she could afford to hire a few key, trusted people.

"I kind of envy you working people," the retiree said. "I miss my job, I do. And so does my wife." He gave a rueful snort of a laugh. "The wife says, and I quote, 'Henry, I married you for better or worse—but not for lunch!'"

Loralie gave a polite smile, and recalled that her mother had reacted much the same way when Loralie's father had retired five years earlier. They had had grand plans for his retirement, but the plans had been cut short when her father had died of a massive coronary. The doctors said the heart attack had robbed him of life almost before he hit the pavement of the hot, downtown Atlanta street. The blistering hot spell was blamed for many deaths, her father's   included.

She and her father had shared many things; numismatics—coin collecting—had been only one of those things. When he had died, she'd assumed that his estate would pass intact to her mother. At the reading of the will, tears came to her eyes when she learned that one-third of Paul Morgan's estate—and his entire coin collection—was her inheritance. With it, came a letter.

Dear Kitten—

Dry those tears, little girl, although I know when you read this letter, your ol' pop will be gone from you. Our good times will always live on, though, won't they?

You know how it was always my dream to become a full-time coin dealer. Different times we talked about going into partnership when I retired. But somehow we never got around to it. I guess it's a dream I'll take to the grave with me.

I know that it was a dream for you too, Lor, and I think it was a real and precious thing, not just an idea you clung to in order to humor your old dad. If it is your dream, sweetheart, then hitch yourself to the nearest star and shoot for the limit.

Your mama and I have talked this over. She's behind you, just like I will be in spirit. My collection will help to create your inventory. (We both know which coins you'll consider "keepers" in my memory, and which ones will do for stock to sell to your customers.)

Good luck, darling girl. You always told me that when it came to being a dad, I was a "slider," ranging from

V-F to X-F. Maybe this'll convince you that I made "full grade." (Just teasing, sweetheart. I know that you considered me tops. So go out there, Loralie, and be the best coin dealer you can, and know that your pop is terribly proud of you.)

It won't be easy for a woman to make it in what is generally considered to be a man's field. I never felt denied that your mama and I didn't have a son, though, because I guess I felt I had the best of both worlds—a beautiful daughter and a "buddy" who was a "chip off the old block."

Love—Dad

P.S. Be friendly, honest, and don't overgrade—and you'll go far in the business, Loralie. The secret to success is to grow bigger by serving better. Never forget that. . . .

Loralie had read her father's last message to her so many times that the words were indelibly imprinted in her mind, and by now, years later, the paper which had been crisp when she'd unfolded the document, was soft, the edges feathery from so much handling. She'd soon realized it could eventually disintegrate beneath her touch, and so she had photocopied it; the original was stored in a plastic sheath to preserve it.

Her thoughts were snapped from the past back to the present when the pilot came on the intercom system again. The aircraft banked as they prepared to come in for a landing. Loralie felt her stomach lurch, and her ears popped from the steep descent. There was a solid jolt as the jet's massive tires hit the paved runway, and Loralie was pushed forward from her seat as the jet braked. Slowly they rolled toward the assigned slot and the pilot nosed his craft into the space. Workers snugged the ramp into place. Passengers stretched, rose, and began collecting their carry-on luggage.

Loralie's aluminum dealer's case was warm where her calf had rested against it. She'd wedged the chunky suitcase-like container between her slim leg and the wall of the aircraft, never letting it out of her sight, nor away from her touch, because it contained almost all that represented her earnings and savings in life.

She hung back, avoiding the crush of disembarking passengers who jammed the center aisle of the craft. The retired businessman, too, remained in his seat, waiting for them to pass. When the aisle was at last clear, he stepped into it, and with a gallant gesture, signalled for Loralie to precede him to the exit doors.

"Thanks." She smiled, and they made small talk as they walked toward the luggage carousel.

Loralie noticed that there were a lot of people

clustered around. Some of them eyed the arriving passengers with the interest of professional people-watchers.

"Have a good flight back to Atlanta," the elderly man said.

"Why, thank you. I'm sure I will."

"Early flight?" he inquired.

"No, later in the day. After the coin show at the Cervantes."

"Good luck," he called over his shoulder.

"Goodbye," Loralie replied.

Gripping the heavy aluminum case that pulled hard at her wrist, elbow, and shoulder, Loralie tried to counter its weight as she hurried to the carousel to claim her lone suitcase. As burdened as she was with her coin inventory, she made it a point to travel light. She carefully chose her clothing when she went on buying trips so she had easy upkeep garments, items that could mix and match to create a myriad of outfits. All could be combined either with the pair of dressy shoes tucked in her suitcase or with the more sensible footwear she had on now.

Her rusty brown hair was cut in a style she could shampoo and push into place with her fingers. It wisped around her face, framing her pert features with burnished copper. Her brown eyes' dark, thick lashes required only a minimum of makeup to create the effect she desired. And with hotel gift shops and notions counters, she didn't bother to pack much; it was easier to overpay for a small, convenience size, and then discard what remained, than to weigh herself down with supplies that she might—or might not—even need.

Loralie's suitcase was not among the other luggage moving around and around on the carousel. She was dismayed, for she'd hoped to exit the doors onto the street and hail a taxi before they were all taken. Now she'd have to wait for a cabby to come to the airport in hopes of a fare.

"Hi!" a fellow near her said. "Going to the show at the Cervantes Convention Center?"

Loralie was a bit surprised. "Yes—but how did you—?"

The words died on her lips when she saw the aluminum dealer's case, a litter mate to hers, positioned solidly between his ankles as the man leaned forward to retrieve his valise.

"You, too?" she inquired politely.

"Uh-huh!" he said, hefting his bag from the claim area.

"Oh! There's mine," Loralie said. "Finally!"

"Let me get it for you," the man offered.

"If you would, that'd be swell."

"Here you go," he said as she accepted the expensive suitcase.

"Where are you staying?" she inquired.

"Right across the street from the Cervantes on Seventh."

"That's where I am too!" Loralie said.

"Want to share a cab?" the dealer asked.

"I'd love to," Loralie agreed, suddenly happy.

She felt as if she had a new friend, a trusted friend—another coin dealer who knew what the business was like, to help her adjust to appearing professionally at her first big show.

"If you'll trust me with your inventory case," the man said, "I'll carry our cases. You can take the lighter suitcases."

Loralie felt a moment's trepidation. She knew a dealer shouldn't let his or her inventory out of his sight and touch, except under extenuating circumstances, like passing through the airport security equipment. But the fellow seemed so nice that she reluctantly let down her guard.

"You've got a deal."

She relinquished her container, noticing that his was as clearly marked with his personal identification as hers, so there'd be no unpleasant mix-up and potential accusations. And, after all, the case was securely locked and its key in her possession.

A cabby hopped from his car and stepped around to open the trunk lid. The tall coin dealer slid the valises into the luggage well. The cabby shot the pair an inquiring look, that seemed to ask if they wanted to surrender the aluminum cases. They shook their heads and walked around to enter the rear seat of the cab.

"So, my name's Jonathan McGuire," the man said.

"Of McGuire Coin Gallery in Boston?" Loralie asked. She couldn't keep the excitement from her voice.

"None other," he replied, smiling in spite of himself at the awe in her tone.

"Wow! I'm honored. Your firm, to me, is right up there with Bower and Merena."

"Well, thank you!" Jonathan said, delight in his voice. "And you might be—?"

"Oh! I'm sorry," Loralie said, blushing over her gaffe. "I'm Loralie Morgan—of Morgan Coins. I have a business in a suburb of Atlanta."

"Pleased to meet you, Loralie Morgan of near-Atlanta. Do you specialize in Morgans?" he inquired, his eyes twinkling.

It was a question she'd been asked, teasingly, many times, especially by collectors who focused on putting together full collections of Morgan Dollars. "Has Loralie Morgan any Morgan Dollars?"

"I have a good inventory," she admitted. "But I serve all needs. I haven't specialized—yet."

"Yet," Jonathan agreed with a smile. "It seems given time, we all narrow our personal focus of interest into a specific coin category that we consider superior to all others. I'm into pattern cents myself."

"Oh, really?" Loralie said.

"I'm getting together with another dealer who has one for sale. If the grade is as good as he says it is, then the price quoted will be fair—and I'll probably acquire another addition for my private collection."

"I had a dealer one time tell me that a person wasn't a true coin dealer unless he or she had *everything* for sale."

"I don't agree," Jonathan said, "although I've been exposed to that sentiment, too."

"My father was a coin collector. And there are some of his especially cherished pieces that I will never sell. Sentimentality adds no value except to the owner, and there isn't enough money to convince me to part with some of those."

"That's how I feel about my pattern pieces. And my Type Set."

"That makes me feel better," Loralie said, and gave a rueful chuckle. "If someone like Jonathan McGuire of McGuire Coin Gallery can retain some unpurchasable favorites without compromising being a 'true' coin dealer, then I guess that I can, too."

Jonathan gave her an amused, but also searching, look. "Are you quite new to the business?"

"I've been doing it several years now. But it's only recently that I've decided to start expanding beyond my local area and the few shows—some of them simply monthly coin club meetings— that I can attend within easy driving distance."

"Great!" Jonathan said. "Welcome to the club of the jet-setting coin dealer. You're going to love it."

"I hope so."

"First show?"

"Uh-huh."

"The Cervantes Convention Center is a great place to start. Wonderful layout. Lovely city. Great and friendly midwestern folks. Agreeable dealers. Tell you what, Loralie, I'll take you around and introduce you to some friends—help get you into the network."

"Would you?" Loralie asked, feeling a bit embarrassed over the plaintive gratitude in her tone; perhaps he would be able to tell just how frightened and insecure and suddenly over-whelmed she felt. "Be glad to. Are you traveling alone?" Jonathan asked.

Loralie nodded.

He frowned. "Got friends in the city? Someone to help—"

"I'm afraid not."

"Most of us travel with a companion. Or else we have local contacts we can rely on."

"I know, but—"

"It's security," Jonathan pointed out. "There are millions of dollars worth of inventory con-tained within that vast room. There are security officers at the doors, and to get in one must sign up and show an ID. But not all coin collectors are honest." He gave a dark frown. "And alas, not all coin dealers are, either."

"I know. I've heard some stories," Loralie admitted. But she hadn't heard anything too terrible, isolated as she'd been, only attending small shows and monthly club meetings. Then the talk had been of an occasional coin filched from a case, palmed by a greedy collector ready to profit at another's expense via theft.

But as Jonathan talked, a chill went through her, for she realized that at the large shows which drew dealers and clientele from every state of the Union, and even from nearby countries, professional thieves either worked alone with a pat routine, or doubled up to create a conspiracy with sleight of hand, state-of-the-art teamwork that could jeopardize the security of even the most watchful and experienced dealers in the field.

"I guess I'll have to keep my eyes open twenty-four hours a day," Loralie mused, hoping she didn't reveal exactly how concerned she had just become. "I have a young assistant back in my area."

She bit back words before she could admit that as new as she was to doing the national shows, and as expensive as it had been to plan the expansion of her business, finances were a decisive factor. For Loralie to fly to the shows now marked on her calendar was costly enough without having to pick up the expenses of an associate.

"You might consider bringing your assistant— and either locking up the shop while you're gone—or expanding your payroll, if you can find a trusted individual to run your enterprise in your absence."

"Advice well given," Loralie said.

"And advice well taken," Jonathan added softly. "Your assistant would probably enjoy it, and it might also increase your dividends. Sometimes at the shows when collectors are stacked up around the table three deep, potential buyers walk away because a lone dealer hasn't the time to service them all. A collector who walks away from your table may well end up buying from a competitor."

"Right you are," Loralie said.

She was glad when the cab arrived at the hotel, and she didn't have to admit to Jonathan McGuire of *the* McGuire Coin Gallery, a huge numismatic concern, that in actuality Morgan Coins was little more than a hole-in-the-wall shop in a low-rent building. And that her "associate" was actually a college fellow, someone other students probably considered "a nerd," a quiet, somewhat odd youth, with a mop of unruly curly hair. He kept his hair that way not because style dictated—but because with his attention riveted on either his engineering program at Georgia Tech or his passion for coin collecting, he simply failed to notice his clean, but scruffy appearance.

Loralie also didn't feel inclined to admit that while she referred to him as "an associate" in the same way that the youth—Jaydee Barton—did her, it was a relationship very loose in structure. They both felt that it gave them a veneer they both needed—and appreciated. While their inventories didn't overlap, a few of their expenses did.

To cut their individual overhead, they had certain shared expenses—and joint services. A post office box. A telephone line rigged so that there were two separate numbers on the same phone, but different rings, signalling when a call was for Jaydee, during his posted hours, and another for Loralie's quite separate business. The shipper they used jointly picked up the items that they directed to clientele across the country, but each dealer kept careful records. Loralie paid for her share of the parcels, Jaydee monitored his own, and their carrier was quite content to accept two checks in payment for the overall bill.

It worked very well, Loralie realized, blending their separate and distinct businesses as they had, but she couldn't imagine herself actually bringing Jaydee to coin shows as an associate. And her contacts were not such, she realized, that she had the network the McGuire Coin Gallery did. If she did, then regardless of what city she traveled to, she could enlist the services of a trusted patron or industry friend to "table sit" for her when she moved around to the tables of other dealers in order to add to her inventory, or seek to find items on various customers' "want lists."

Jonathan helped Loralie from the taxi that double-parked in front of the hotel and hastened to fetch their luggage. With her newly-trained eyes, she recognized another incoming coin dealer, obviously in the Gateway City for the same show she and Jonathan were attending. In tow was a beautifully and expensively dressed woman and a teenage son.

"Perhaps what I need is a wife," Loralie joked.

Even at the small monthly meetings, the male dealers who had a wife present were at an advantage. Even if a dealer's mate was relatively ignorant about the ins and outs of numismatics and couldn't tell a Barber dime from the common-issue Roosevelt variety, her presence was valuable.

"I've thought of that option, too," Jonathan said, laughing along with Loralie. "But I know the Lord wouldn't want me to settle for any woman, just to get a pretty and agreeable 'table sitter'. I haven't met the woman meant for me, so it seems, and when I do, she'll be the one God has planned for me. Then it'll be a true partnership in all ways. Not a convenient. . .business arrangement."

For a moment Loralie's heart skipped a beat, then soared with sudden euphoria. She'd had no idea that Jonathan McGuire was a committed Christian. She wondered if that was why she had felt drawn to him—trusted him—because their unspoken faith had drawn them together, linking them in their love of the Lord, even though they'd only met moments before.

"That's how I feel, too," Loralie said. She couldn't help entertaining a surge of relief that the handsome Boston businessman was not married.

"The fare's on me," Jon said, turning to attend to the cab driver's financial needs.

"Okay. But only if you let me take care of the tip," Loralie said.

Jon seemed to hesitate for a moment. Then he nodded agreement. "Okay."

She smiled, relieved that he allowed her to perform as she desired and didn't patronize her as a female. She was nervously aware that she was about to enter a professional business arena overwhelmingly populated by hard-bargaining, perhaps even good-ol'-boy-network men.

But with a friend like Jonathan—and another Friend in her Savior, a Person known to both of them—Loralie knew a wonderful surge of confident serenity.

The St. Louis show was going to be *great*!

two

Loralie and Jonathan queued up in line to transact the business needed to attend to their hotel reservations. To Loralie's relief, it went off without a hitch. A few minutes later, she headed to the bank of elevators, the plastic "key" clutched in her fingers. The bell captain carried her valise, while she insisted she keep possession of her aluminum coin case.

"This is a lovely hotel," Loralie said, making conversation.

"We're proud of it," the attractive, immaculately uniformed hotel employee said. "Your room has a super view of the Arch."

"It's quite a landmark, isn't it?" Loralie said.

With civic pride, the employee began to rattle off the statistics, how long the famous aluminum Gateway Arch had taken for its construction, what amount of materials had been required, the dimensions, and the fact that sometimes stunt flyers flew between the "legs" of the arch, much like a ball went through a croquet wicket.

"There are tours. You can take an elevator to the top of the Arch," he said. "The view from that point is terrific—at least on a sunny day. When St. Louis is shrouded in fog it might be a disappointment."

"Maybe I'll find time to do it when I'm in the city," Loralie mused.

"Plan to allow a couple of hours—to wait in line—being as you're in St. Louis approaching the weekend. Through the week the wait's not so lengthy."

"I guess that's out, then," Loralie said. "I can't allow that kind of time." Nor, she thought, could she leave her coin inventory, nor wish to carry it into what was such a crowded place with no real security.

"There are museums on the lower level," the man said. "They're worth seeing. They have done a superlative job of collecting interesting items for viewing. There are videos, live cultural performances, and more."

"Sounds great. St. Louis really offers a lot, doesn't it?"

"More than many people realize. The Forest Park Zoo is rated among the best in the United States. It's incredible. And not far from the zoo is the Science Center."

Enthusiastically, he described the computer areas, the prehistoric displays of life-size dinosaurs locked in killing battle, the space exhibitions, the geological displays. "And what's wonderful is that it's free to the public. They have a container to accept donations, but no one is barred for financial reasons from enjoying all it offers."

"A person I met at the airport told me how great midwesterners are," Loralie said. "And your city certainly seems to reflect that attitude."

"We have a lot more—the Botanical Gardens, Busch Stadium where the Cardinals' baseball games are played. The St. Louis arena where the Blues play hockey. The Checker Dome. Union Station. And St. Louis is considered a medical center, too, with Barnes, Children's, Jewish, Glennon, St. Louis University Hospitals—and a host of others. There's a lot of research done here. We have an eye specialist doing cutting-edge research in vision diseases. Among his colleagues the world over he's referred to as 'The Retina King.' Our hospitals are internationally famous."

"That's nice to know," Loralie said, "although I certainly hope I won't require any health care services during my stay."

"That's our wish for you, too, ma'am." The bell captain accepted the plastic planchet from Loralie, opened her room, and turned on the lights as she fished into her pocketbook for a tip.

With a smile he discreetly accepted it. "Enjoy your stay, ma'am. And if you need anything—just call down to the desk. We're here to make your visit as pleasurable as possible."

And profitable, too, Loralie thought, as she closed her door behind the bell captain and secured it. Only then did she set her inventory case on the bed, letting it out of her sight and grip.

A moment later Loralie's stomach growled,

and she realized she was famished. With what Jon had said about the need for security, however, she suddenly felt a prickle of alarm at the idea of going out for dinner. Her arm ached from bearing the weight of her inventory, for the case probably weighed close to forty or fifty pounds, as solidly filled as it was with numismatic items. She didn't know if she could bear lugging it with her to a restaurant. And she quailed at the idea of leaving it in her hotel room.

She quickly ruled out that option. She'd made her reservation—as had Jon and many others—under the special discount offered to attend the coin show at the Cervantes Convention Center. That meant the hotel employees would be able to easily guess what the metal case contained. She realized that by and large the hotel's employees could be trusted, but all it would take would be one mercenary employee to do a surreptitious check—or worse, a quick printout—and persons with devious and deceptive plans could know exactly in what rooms dealers were staying.

While the plastic planchets made the doors relatively secure, if an employee could be swayed by the right price, she was all too aware that a quick in-and-out of her room could rob her of her worldly investments.

It wasn't like her to distrust people—but she knew that as she walked through the world, she had to think of how those guided by worldly principles, not Christian values, might behave.

She had to take measures in order not to lead them into temptation. And if she didn't, she set herself up for professional destruction.

Loralie drifted across the room to the desk where a telephone book, fire escape card, and several other standard hotel notification cards were neatly arranged on the surface. She selected the room service menu, swallowed hard over the prices, and considered what she'd like to order.

She was surprised when the telephone less than two feet away from her shrilled. For a moment her pulse thudded. She had no idea who to expect. Perhaps it was a wrong number.

"Hello?"

"Loralie? Jon."

"Oh. . .hi!"

"Are you about settled in?"

"Getting there," she replied. "I've been looking over my room."

"My quarters are superb."

"Same here. I was about to consider unpacking. You caught me just as I was scanning the room service menu card."

"Ordered yet?"

"No."

"Great. That's what I was calling about. I didn't plan ahead and make any dinner dates with coin dealing buddies who've also come to town. I'm free, and if you are, too, I'd love to have you accompany me."

"That sounds good," Loralie said.

She was about to wonder aloud what to do about her inventory case, but then Jon attended to that consideration before she could raise it. "The Cervantes is open. I was thinking that if you're agreeable, we could meet in the lobby in a few minutes, cut across to the Cervantes, show our dealer passes to the security guards at the door, and go in and drop off our cases at our allotted tables. Then we wouldn't have to have back-of-the-mind security worries, and we could relax and enjoy an evening out on the town."

"That sounds absolutely wonderful," Loralie breathed, relieved.

"We could return early enough to get back to the Cervantes to set up our tables tonight so that everything would be ready to go when the doors open to the public in the morning."

"You won't hear any arguments from me," Loralie said. "That plan is super."

"How long do you need?" Jon asked. "I've heard stories about you women—"

Loralie gave a comfortable chuckle. "I'm not like other women," she said. "Give me two minutes. Five at most."

"You *are* different," Jonathan teased. "Should I call the Guiness People?"

"If you like," Loralie bantered back. "But if you do, I hope they don't put you on hold so you keep *me* waiting!"

"See you in the lobby!"

"Bye!" Loralie said.

Quickly, she hung up the telephone, riffled a comb through her hair, applied fresh makeup, straightened her clothing, and concluded that she looked decidedly presentable. When she and Jon entered the lobby at the same time, she saw from the admiring look in his eyes that she presented a most attractive appearance.

"Let me carry the cases," he said. "It's several blocks to the door we're supposed to use."

"Okay," she agreed. "But it does seem unfair to have you lug around my heavy case."

"You'll be happier if we have an equal division of labor?"

She nodded.

"What are you?" he teased. "A feminist?"

"No, not really." She didn't bother to explain that while she believed in some of the issues for women's rights, her Christian principles caused her to reject just as many. "Just a woman who is wishing to make it in a man's world, without others saying that unfair allowances were made based on gender alone."

"And there might be some who'll say that," Jon said, giving a frown. "You'll probably run into some men who won't give you the helping hand they'd naturally extend to another man, simply because you are a woman. And a very attractive woman."

"I'd feared as much."

"But far be it from me to be patronizing or condescending, my dear," he assured. "I must admit that I like your attitude and your desire to make it in a man's world with no excuses given, nor apologies required. I respect that you want to perform your duties by yourself. Even so, I insist on carrying this heavy case. But I can, and will, parcel out your duties in this business arrangement. There's something you can do."

"Name it," Loralie said.

"You can hold the doors for me."

Loralie smiled. "I'd expected to."

He grinned. "I had a hunch you'd say that. And before we step onto the street, I want to delineate our mutual responsibilities."

"Okay. . . ." Loralie solemnly said, waiting for instructions.

"If we should happen to be accosted by the thugs, my efforts will be to fight them off—and your responsibilities will be to scream the skyscrapers down."

"Agreed," Loralie said, extending her hand.

Jonathan hefted their aluminum cases. "You'll just have to take my word of honor. I'm not letting these babies out of my grip until we relinquish them to the care of the security force at the Center."

For a moment Loralie fell into shaken, almost chastened silence when she considered the differences between their inventories, carried in cases that were almost exact duplicates except for their identity information and their individual scuffs and dents. True, she had valuable and very collectible numismatic items in her case, but their total value might easily be equaled with just a few coins that Jonathan, should he care to do so, could carry in an inner pocket of his tailored suit coat.

Loralie carried quite a lot of gold coinage, but she had no true rarities. She simply couldn't afford to sock those kinds of funds into individual items at this time, although she hoped and dreamed that day would come. Her inventory ran more to silver and copper, with her dealing in basically high grade coins, and key date items in nothing under V-F.

A shiver went through her when she realized that contained within her case was inventory retailing at several hundred thousand dollars. But in Jon's case that he carried just as carefully as hers was coin stock with individual values of sometimes thirty thousand dollars—or more. She could actually be walking down Seventh Street with a man worth millions.

But something told her that Jonathan McGuire didn't put all that much value in material things. Like she, he knew that the true thing of worth, the most rare and precious possession in the world, was the Christian faith.

He'd tipped his hand to her so that she knew of his convictions. She couldn't help wondering, with a ripple of excitement, what his reaction would be when he realized that not only did they share the lore of numismatics, but they also held in common a love and faith in Jesus Christ.

"I thought that if it's all right with you, after we stow our possessions at our tables, we'd go to The Spaghetti Factory. It's got a rep in this area. They serve more than pasta, of course, but their Italian dishes are their forte."

"Ah, the answer to prayer," Loralie said. "I was almost fantasizing about pasta when I was scanning the room service menu. The idea of exemplary pasta has my mouth watering."

"Great! I'll enjoy exposing you to one of the best places to eat our kind of food while in St. Louis."

As kind as Jon had been to her, Loralie felt a twinge of desire to insist that their dinner would be her treat. He must have read her thoughts in her expression, though, for he quickly added, "And before you can whip out your wallet, my dear, as quick as a deadbeat in the face of a loan shark's enforcer, get it through your pretty head that *tonight* is on me."

Loralie was thoughtful. "Very well," she agreed, her heartbeat suddenly escalating, "but only if some night this week when you're free, we can perhaps share another meal—and it'll be *my* treat."

Jonathan gave her a rakish grin, laughing softly at the way she had reversed the stereotypical gender roles. "I thought you'd never ask. I'd love to! I've enjoyed doing 'business' with you, Miss Loralie," Jon said. "So let's dispense with our inventories, and grab a cab and head for The

Spaghetti Factory to do some pleasure. You're a charming and wonderful companion."

"Ditto," Loralie said lightly. "I'm so glad I met you."

Meeting him, she realized, was like an answer to prayer. No, it wasn't *like* an answer to prayer, it *was* an answer to prayer. Continuing proof that the Lord God saw to her needs, sometimes even before she recognized them. He brought the right people and events into her life that she might learn lessons in wisdom and mature as a Christian. All the experiences she encountered—good, bad, or indifferent—helped shape her into the Christian woman that God wished her to be.

three

"Oh, Jonathan, this has been one of the most exquisite meals of my entire life. I was famished, too," she said, giving a rueful gesture that took in the assortment of empty plates that the waiter was deftly clearing away. "I had a bagel on the way out the door when I left my apartment this morning, but that's all I'd eaten today."

"I did the chef's efforts proud, myself," he agreed.

"Cappuccino?" the waiter inquired.

Jonathan nodded and held up two fingers.

"I'm glad I let you order for me," Loralie said. "Somehow I knew that I could trust your judgment."

Jonathan gave a careless shrug. "I know what I like—in coins and companionship."

Loralie felt her face warm with a blush. "Thank you. I assume that was a compliment?"

"Of the most sincere kind."

"I'm really glad that I signed up to attend this show," Loralie said. "Because of you it's going to be a wonderful experience. Making my initial contact with the national coin network is going to be special because of the part you're playing in it."

"Have you business cards?" Jonathan inquired.

"Of course."

"I'd figured as much, but I meant a goodly supply."

Loralie nodded. Her cards had cost her more than many people might consider reasonable, but she knew that it was a wise and prudent expense, even if her cards had been among the most expensive that the local printer had prepared.

Many times over the years her father had said that even though material things were not important, in some ways they were. He'd offered the twinkling-eyed explanation that if you had to choose a lawyer to represent a legal case, you would probably have more confidence in an attorney who drove a top-of-the-line Cadillac than one who drove an ancient car.

"You only have one chance to make a good first impression, Kitten," he'd reminded. "So do it with your appearance and your actions."

Loralie had believed her father was right. As a result she'd spared no expense in having her business cards, letterhead, and other office incidentals prepared. She'd also inquired around and retained the services of the best sign painting shop for the windows to her shop. She considered herself fortunate that a friend from high school, Janeen, was in the interior decoration business and had offered her opinion and a few services free as she helped Loralie plan the layout and atmosphere for her coin shop.

"I'm glad you came prepared with business cards," Jonathan said.

"Why?"

He paused. "I thought that if you were willing, I'd take a few, have you write your table number on the back, and I'd pass them out to a few dealer friends of mine."

"That's generous of you."

"It might help your profit line a bit," he admitted. "If you can introduce yourself as a personal friend of mine, and I've distributed a few of your cards to pave the way, they might give you an added break on any merchandise you're interested in acquiring."

"And I will be purchasing quite a lot of numismatic stock," Loralie admitted. In her case were both her business checkbook, and a large sum of cash, as some people preferred cash-on-the-barrelhead dealings when they bought or sold. "I can't express how much this means to me."

"Glad to do it," Jonathan said.

But why? Loralie almost blurted before she stemmed the words. In her woman's heart, she sensed she knew the answer to that. Jonathan respected her as a professional in the field. Clearly, he enjoyed her company. But more than that . . .she sensed he was attracted to her as a woman.

Was he, too, wondering if she was the woman meant for him? The mate ordained by a loving God? Had she, in little ways, given away the

Christian commitment that she tried her best to live on a daily basis? Had he detected the little remarks and mannerisms that allowed one Christian to recognize another?

"Well, well, well!" a loud voice boomed, shattering the tender moment of Loralie's musings. "Who have we here? And what are we seeing him with?!"

Loralie craned around, wondering who was so boisterously speaking within the pleasant, convivial, and socially refined atmosphere. She didn't realize that the loud stranger who approached their table was speaking to Jonathan until he bypassed the group of diners at the nearby table. As he drew alongside the table for two, Jonathan arose, extending his hand.

"Denis St. John! How are you? I haven't seen you since. . .when? Seattle? Or was it Dallas?"

"Wrong on both counts, my man," Mr. St. John said. "I remember us passing in the main area of JFK airport in New York. But it was such fleeting contact that I won't hold it against you that you've forgotten."

"Right you are. Sorry, Denny. Would you care to join us?" Jonathan politely asked, even though there really wasn't room. Loralie realized, though, that a waiter could crowd another chair to the table if the customers so desired.

"No, no, Jon." St. John cast Loralie a glance— one that was difficult to read. "It appears that you're. . .occupied . . .for the evening."

"Oh, excuse me, Loralie, Denny." Jonathan paused. "Loralie, this is Denis St. John. Denny, please meet one of the Atlanta area's loveliest belles, Ms. Loralie Morgan."

"Pleased to meet you," Loralie said, extending her hand as she offered a pleasant smile.

The glowering man regarded her hand as if he wasn't quite sure what to do with it, then reluctantly extended his grip, which she found as cold and harsh as were his incredibly handsome features.

"Likewise," he said in a curt tone.

"Loralie's setting up at the Cervantes Center along with the rest of us," Jonathan said. Loralie realized he was attempting to get the conversation off and rolling. So she opted to do her part.

"I'm really looking forward to it. It's my first big show."

"I didn't think I'd heard the name. Or seen the face around," St. John said.

"Well, remember the name, and I'm sure you'll have no trouble remembering the face. In my opinion, I think she has the makings to create a major reputation in the field."

"Are you setting up at the bourse?" Loralie asked of Denis St. John.

"No, I'm here in another professional capacity."

"Have a good flight in?" Jonathan inquired, when he seemed to sense, along with Loralie, that there was a cold, unfriendly edge to the tall man's tone.

"I always have a good flight. I have my pilot's license and bought a new Cessna last year. I don't travel commercial liners any more except in an emergency. My business schedule is such that it saves me time. Plus, I don't have to contend with the flight attendants' interruptions—causing me a disturbance—and ruining my thoughts, as they solicitously inquire about my 'comfort'."

What a thoroughly disagreeable man, Loralie thought. She felt a bit of surprise that Jon was so patient and pleasant to him, apparently accepting his almost antisocial behavior with good grace and tolerance.

"I failed to mention, Loralie, that Denny is an important man in the world of numismatics. I'm sure you've read articles by him, and profiles about him. He's a counterfeit detection expert. He works with the ANA in Colorado, the PNG, and he belongs to a host of professional organizations—the LSCC, the JRSC. You name it— and our man, Denny, more than likely currently belongs—or once was a charter member."

"Well. . .I'm impressed," Loralie murmured, not sure if the tone would be construed as sincere or sarcastic, because she wasn't quite sure of the verdict herself.

From what Jon had said, Loralie was aware that Denis St. John belonged to the American Numismatics Association, the Professional Numismatists Guild, the Liberty Seated Coin Club, the

John Reich Collectors Society and a host of other professional organizations.

"You must belong to everything," Loralie said, trying for a decidedly admiring tone when a prickly silence stretched among them.

"Just about. I refuse to join a church—*or* NOW."

His voice was cutting, and she wasn't sure if the religious slur was an insult sent in Jon's direction, and the reference to women's issues a slur toward her. But what she did know was that beneath his handsome smile and polished appearance, Denis St. John had the capacity to be a very nasty man.

"I don't belong to NOW, either, if that's any reassurance to you," Loralie found herself saying, even as she didn't want to. "But I am a member of a lovely little wood and stone church, and of the Body of Christ, created by the unification of all believers in their faith and trust in Jesus Christ."

Denis said nothing. His lip that curled into a sneer said quite enough. . . .

"What's his problem?" Loralie inquired when Denis St. John had moved away, and she could whisper the words to her dinner companion.

"I'm not sure. To him, religion is anathema. Not sure why. And, he's something of a misogynist. That, I can pinpoint to a past relationship that devastated him and caused him to distrust all women."

"The understatement of the year. I think his picture could serve as the dictionary illustration to accompany the listing for 'male chauvinist pig.'"

Jon gave a hearty laugh. "Loralie Morgan, you are a treasure. A rare and precious woman."

"And at risk of seeming forward, Jon, I am forming the same impression about you."

"We both seemed to have impressed one another," he admitted.

"My father always said an individual only had one chance to make a good first impression. Apparently we each did well for ourselves. Now . . .as to Denis St. John. . . ."

"Don't judge him too harshly, Lor," Jon murmured. "He's an easy man for many people to hate. I get along with him quite well. But I'm tolerant, even sympathetic. For I realize that without the Lord. . .there but for the grace of God could walk I."

"I suppose," Loralie agreed. "I hadn't really thought about that."

"I have. And I think there's a wonderful man beneath that rough, gruff, vindictive, vitriolic surface."

"It would take the armor of a Sherman Tank to withstand the efforts needed to unearth it. . . ."

"I quite agree. But, we possess an even better armor. We have the shield of the Lord. Try not to hate Denis St. John. Try to be willing to pray for him instead. No matter what he does. . . ."

The last words were delivered in a calm manner, but they sent a chill through Loralie. She'd seen the look in Denis St. John's eyes. His cold stare had seemed a challenge—and a warning—that he would love nothing better than to destroy her not only professionally, but personally as well.

Was Jonathan trying to alert her to the fact that the only way she'd survive was if she took advantage of the Lord's protection, and allowed Him to shield her, keeping herself safe from Denis St. John's human potential to reach her if she kept herself hidden in Him?

Time—and tomorrow—would surely tell.

four

Loralie was yawning when she and Jon entered the Cervantes Convention Center from one of the Seventh Street entrances and showed their dealer pass identification cards to the armed officer in charge of security clearances. More dealers had arrived, and the room was a hive of activity as dealers from across the continental United States were calling out cheerful greetings to one another as they arranged their stalls.

Loralie's booth was in the 600's, and Jon's was in the 700's. But the arrangements of the spaces resulted in them being back-to-back with Jon about halfway down the long aisle from her. If they both turned at the same time, they could make eye contact.

Loralie had only rented one table, and had spoken for two of the rental display cases. Jon had spoken for three tables and half a dozen cases.

Loralie swallowed hard as she paid the case rental fee, for she had cases in her shop that were duplicates, but entirely too bulky to consider shipping, even though the rental fee per case totaled about one-fourth of the price of a new case.

"It's one way for the local club to make some

money," Jon had said, and Loralie agreed with him. Plus, the convenience of not shipping cases that were two and a half feet wide by almost four feet long, with glass tops, made it worthwhile.

When Loralie had finished arranging her items for display, she unfolded a cloth with *Morgan Coins* emblazoned on it and spread it across the top of the cases to shroud the display. To the rear of her booth, hanging by wires from steel piping, was the calligraphy sign announcing her booth number and her business name. She set a little plastic display rack of business cards in a strategic location on the table top and considered the job done.

She'd promised Jon that she'd meet him at his booth when she had finished, so that he could accompany her along the late night street to their hotel. He, however, had experienced so many interruptions due to dealer friends stopping by to say hello and pass a bit of time, that he'd not finished his work.

"Need some help?" Loralie asked.

Jon gave a groan. "If you don't mind, I could use a hand."

"Tell me what to do."

"You've done this countless times," he said casually. "Just go for it. I won't complain."

Loralie worked quietly and efficiently. Several times more Jon was taken away from his activities to perform the social aspects of their profession.

"Who's the pretty lady? Found yourself a 'table-sitter,' have you? Be sure to let us know when the date is you're going to make it official . . . ."

Loralie blushed when she realized that they'd assumed that she was Jon's girlfriend, perhaps en route to becoming his wife.

"She's pretty enough to nicely decorate a dealer's booth as a mere table sitter. But make no mistake, Loralie's one of us, guys!" Quickly Jon made more introductions.

Loralie noticed that in the numismatic field, Jon's word was gold—just like the many rare coins he offered. And to most of his friends, his acceptance of her as a peer was good enough for them.

Only one man had reacted differently—Denis St. John—who for some reason, had seemed to resent her, and resent her deeply, the very moment he'd laid eyes on her.

But why? Loralie wondered, as she excused herself while Jon finished up the last touches to his allotted space. She made her way down the long hallway and around a corner to the rest rooms. She whisked a comb through her hair and touched up her lipstick, immediately rearranging her face when she saw her frown reflected in the mirror. Denis St. John's reaction had somehow seemed as much . . .*personal* as it had obviously been professional.

It was puzzling. She knew that he seemed to

resent and dislike her. But she had no understanding of why. And she didn't know if she could candidly and tactfully broach the issue with Jon, a man who seemed to like and enjoy her as much as Denis St. Jon most certainly did not. . . .

"I'm ready if you are," Jon called out as Loralie approached. When she drew near, he disengaged himself from the cluster of coin dealers, all men, whom she'd met earlier. "Shall we go, my dear?" Jon asked with a joking attitude of excruciatingly correct gallantry, and offered her his elbow.

"Posthaste," Loralie bantered back and looped her arm through his. Together they strolled away from the group, but not before Loralie overheard the remarks.

"Stunning couple, aren't they?"

"Old J.P. McGuire's son may've met his match this time. . . ."

"And here we thought he was 'married' to his business."

"Don't give up on him yet, boys. It'll take one very special woman to convince Jonny McGuire to exchange golden coins for a plain gold band . . . ."

"Who is she?"

"Some girl from the Atlanta area, didn't Jon say?"

"A coin dealer, no less."

"Well, certainly as pretty to the eye as that honeyed drawl is appealing to the ears."

Loralie, realizing that Jon overheard, too,

decided to respond, rather than walk on in rigid silence, pretending not to have heard.

She squeezed his arm and gave a faint giggle. "Fiddle-dee-dee!" she whispered.

Jon threw back his head and laughed. "And spoken in a manner to perfectly rival Miss Scarlett."

"Why thank you, *suh*. . . ."

"I promise you, Miss Loralie, you're going to be the belle of the bourse tomorrow. Just be yourself, and everyone will adore you. They won't be able to help themselves. Your feminine wiles could beguile them—but your charms won't have to—for the quality of your merchandise will."

"I hope so," Loralie said.

"Some of my dealer friends were looking over your shoulder. Knowing that we were friends, they took it upon themselves to rather clandestinely report back. You have already developed a reputation, my dear."

"And—?"

"A good one, never fear. They all think that you've got a tremendous eye for detail, and that when it comes to grading coins, you're a real straight arrow. Word will get around that you're honest, upright, and that you grade accurately, and knowing you, price accordingly."

"I try."

"Not only do you try, Loralie, but you succeed. Just keep it up, never sacrifice your ethics, and your business will expand along the very lines you desire."

"You remind me of my father. Not in looks," Loralie quickly explained, "but in philosophy." Hastily she extracted the business cards she'd withheld for Jon, after writing her booth number on the reverse. "This," she pointed to a line in flowing script near the bottom of the business card, "was something that my father frequently impressed upon me."

Jon looked at the sentiment. *Growing bigger by serving better.* "I couldn't agree more," he said as they stepped outside into the cool night.

With their hands unencumbered by cases, Jon took Loralie's in his, and they leisurely strolled toward the hotel.

"Could I interest you in a cup of coffee, soft drink, or juice in the hotel dining room?"

"Jon, I'd really love to. Truly I would. But it's getting so late. I have to arise early tomorrow."

"I'm not easily daunted, dear girl. Shall we make it breakfast, then? I could insure that you arrive safely within the confines of the Cervantes Convention Center at the appointed hour."

"You've got a date," Loralie said.

"And while I'm at it, maybe I should press for a further commitment. You said something about taking me out for dinner. Are we on for tomorrow night?"

"Of course. If you've nothing better to do, I'd love it."

"No matter what options could tempt, Loralie, there's nothing in the world that I'd consider an improvement over spending an evening with you."

"It's a date then," Loralie said happily. "Another date. I'll let you select the restaurant, since you know the Gateway City far better than I."

"I know it'll be a special evening regardless of where we dine."

Jon walked Loralie to the bank of elevators. For a moment she thought he was going to shake her hand. Then she almost feared that he was going to bring his lips to hers, even though they'd just met that very afternoon. She found that she felt a heady blend of both excitement and alarm. Then she chided herself that they had a relationship, yes, but she really wasn't sure if it was on a business level or personal.

"Why not both?" she murmured as she stepped off the elevator on the top floor. She'd no sooner rounded a corner to head toward her room than she collided with a tall, solid form. A muttered oath grated against her ears. She winced, even as she was about to frame a polite apology.

Before she could, a voice was harsh near her ear. "You! It's *you!*"

She stared up into the eyes of Denis St. John, who, without Jonathan's restraining presence, seemed to look at her with an even more livid look.

"Is there no getting away from you?" he

demanded to know. "What are you doing? Following me like some kind of-of. . .coin-collecting groupie?"

"I beg your pardon," Loralie said so coldly that it reversed the meaning of her remark, "but my room is on this floor. Now if you'll excuse me—!"

She sidestepped around Denis St. John.

But he was not about to allow it. He grabbed her arm. "Lady, I don't know what you're up to—"

"I have no idea what you're up to, either, Mr. St. John. But if you don't remove your hands from me right this minute, I'm going to scream the roof down, report you to security, and—"

"You'd do it, too, wouldn't you?" he inquired, his eyes narrowing.

"You'd better believe that I would. So don't push me, buster," Loralie warned, feeling her rare temper mounting. "Powerful things come in small packages—like dynamite—so don't throw your weight around!"

"You know, Ms. Morgan, in this business my word means a lot. With a few discreet remarks dropped in the right places—I could make you or break you."

For a response Loralie gave a helpless, bitter laugh, which she could tell infuriated Denis St. John who was accustomed to having persons cater to him, solicitously seeking to serve his needs and soothe his ego. "You can't make or break me, you egotistical, foul-tempered, rude-mannered Boor of the Bourse!"

"Oh yeah?"

"Yes!"

"Says who?"

"Says *me*!"

"And just what does a simple-minded southern belle, who fancies herself a coin dealer, know about what Denis St. John can or cannot do?"

"There are certain things that I know beyond doubt, Mr. St. John," Loralie said in a crisp tone. Suddenly she felt a calm sweep over her, and she was grateful when her tone changed from shaky to serene and well-modulated, with just a trace of her drawl evident. "I know that you don't possess all the power you'd like people to believe that you do. I know that you're just a man. No better, or no worse, than any other sinner on earth."

"Sinner?" the man yelped. "You have the audacity to label me a *sinner*?! Young lady, your lawyer may be hearing from *my* lawyer over that one."

Without flinching, Loralie presented the name of the legal firm in Atlanta who represented her. She almost laughed when she saw the degree to which that tactic took the wind from Denis St. John's sails.

"We're all sinners, Mr. St. John. But not all of us are aware of it and feel convicted by our shortcomings. I freely admit my status as a sinner in need of the Lord's redemption. You'd be a much happier man if you would—"

When she saw he was about to have a stroke from the anger her words were raising in him, she realized she had to quickly let him know she could withstand whatever he sent in her direction.

"I'm sure it pleases you to believe you have the power to make or break men—and women," Loralie chided. "But that's only your fantasy. The fact is that God is sovereign. Nothing will happen to me—you won't touch so much as a hair on my head—except that the Lord will allow it . . .so that *His* needs are served, and my Christian life perfected." She paused. "You may think that you do your own will, and maybe you do, Denis St. John, but a wise, all-powerful, and all-knowing Creator, who knows you and loves you as thoroughly and completely as He does Jon and me, can use your cruelty and your weaknesses that others might be strengthened in their walk with Him."

"You're insane, lady! You're a fruitcake! You should probably be locked up in an asylum, wrapped in a strait jacket—instead of designer clothes—and the key to your cell thrown away."

For three full minutes, Loralie let him rant on. People on the same floor eventually stuck their heads out their doors, ordered the man to shut up with his tirade, and warned that if he didn't they were going to call security and have him removed.

"More people over whom you seem to have no miraculous powers to impress," Loralie murmured.

Denis St. John gave her a murderous look.

His temper drew a second wind, and he was about to begin a fresh recitation, but Loralie casually walked away.

"Sorry to disappoint you, but I can no longer agree to be your captive audience of one. It's late, and I've got a coin show to attend in the morning. Why don't you go to your room and put your temper and ego to bed? You might try awakening quietly in the morning—so you can arise and slip away without your ego and temper knowing and accompanying you across the street."

"You really think you're a cute and classy dame, don't you?" Denis said, his tone louder than he probably realized. "Well, I think—"

His raging torrent of words was cut short by Loralie's wide grin.

"What are you smirking about?" he demanded to know.

"I gave you the name of my attorney, Mr. St. John. Would you consider doing the same? Because if you don't refrain from speaking about me in public in the manner that you are—it could quickly become a case where *my* lawyer will end up seeking to speak with *your* lawyer."

"Pushy dame!" Denis growled as he turned on his heel.

"See you tomorrow!" Loralie called after him in a pleasant tone.

"Not if I see you first. . . ."

His response was surly, and oddly enough, defeated. Being bested was not something he tolerated well.

As Loralie unlocked her hotel room door, she couldn't help feeling a sense of foreboding envelop her. She knew that Denis St. John would never triumph over the Lord's protection of her. But she was only human, and she suffered a prickling tingle of alarm when she considered what he'd do if he waged a battle of evil to try to destroy her good name in the business. . . .

five

The next morning Loralie awoke even before the desk clerk could ring her room with the wake-up call she'd requested the night before. She didn't arise immediately, though. Instead, she drifted in a place between sleep and wakefulness, her thoughts chaotic, as she thought ahead toward her day, while at the same time reflecting back over the day and evening before.

"Thanks!" Loralie said when her bedside telephone shrilled, and she knew it was time to rise and shine for the day.

She hastened through her morning routine—showering, using the hotel's blow dryer, and quickly applying makeup. She was just putting on her simple gold jewelry, austere compared to what some dealers wore, when her telephone rang again.

"Lor? Jon. About ready to head for the coffee shop?"

"Just waiting for your call. I'm all ready to go."

"And some men complain how long it takes women to get ready!"

"Some women. Not this one. I try to travel through life light—and simply."

"So I'd noticed. Maybe that's your real appeal.

You're an interesting—but uncomplicated—female."

"Denis St. John would certainly beg to disagree with you."

Jon paused. "He really got through to you, didn't he? Touched a raw nerve."

Loralie was thoughtful. "No, not really. At least not for me. But it would seem that perhaps I have an inborn talent for causing him to react as if nails had been scraped across a blackboard."

"C'mon. Go easy on yourself. You're not that bad. And really, he's not either. Once you get used to him."

Loralie gave a snort. "Quite frankly, I doubt that I shall live long enough to ever get accustomed to one Denis St. John."

"Whew! There were obviously more sparks flying between you two than I noticed. And here I had a ringside seat at The Spaghetti Factory."

"Then you should've been on the elevator after I went up from the lobby."

"You had another encounter with Denny?"

"None other."

"Do tell, Loralie. . . ."

"It wasn't pleasant."

"How unpleasant was it?"

"Well, initially, he began to rail at me and threatened that his lawyer would end up talking to my lawyer. Then I gave him as good as he was giving—in a more ladylike and less obnoxious manner, I might point out. I finally decided I'd had all that I could take. So I requested the name of his lawyer in order that my lawyer could be in touch. . .!"

Jonathan laughed. "I'll bet that went over like a lead balloon."

"The understatement of the year."

"So then what happened?"

"His parting sentiment was that he could make or break me, and that he was going to make it his point to avoid me. That I wouldn't be seeing him—not if he spotted me first."

"Count your blessings if he's planning on avoiding you, my dear."

Silence stretched between them.

"What do you mean by that comment?"

A longer silence seemed to express that Jonathan realized he'd spoken rashly and regretted that he had, but knew it was too late to bite back the words.

"Denny's had his vendettas. He's a great one to try to manipulate everyone into taking up sides. He's in. At this point, you're really, unfortunately. . .not. Our boy Denny could be planning to really 'settle your hash' by arranging for this to be your first, last, and only show."

"Jon, is he really that bad?"

"Oh, sometimes even worse," he assured with almost joyous tones, as if to try to convince Loralie that Denny certainly wasn't planning dastardly deeds for her like he had for some. "But let's talk about it over breakfast, Lor. I'm sure you'll feel better if you're not famished."

"Okay. Race you to the table," she challenged as she hung up.

Jon arrived a split second before Loralie, so they were seated at a table for two, and the waitress brought them coffee to enjoy while they scanned the menu and made their choices.

"I'm scared," Loralie finally admitted. "I suppose that I really shouldn't have challenged Mr. St. Denis. Maybe I wouldn't have if I'd really known exactly who he is."

"That was the richest comeuppance I've ever seen." Jonathan assured. "Denny's so positive everyone is aware of his reputation of renown that I wouldn't have missed it for the world to have seen his ego deflated when you didn't know every jot and tittle of his accomplishments and credentials within the industry."

"He's eminently qualified," she had to admit.

"More so than you're even aware. In addition to the groups I listed last night, he's also affiliated with ANE, IRCS, PCGS, NSDR, and writes regularly for both *Coin World* and *Numismatic News Weekly*, with occasional pieces in *Coin Age*."

"How depressing. . . ."

"But that should reassure you about his professionalism, dear girl. . . ."

"As a coin dealer and collector, yes. But I'm afraid it does nothing to reassure me of his ethics as a human being."

Jon was silent a long time. He looked as though he were mentally riffling through past incidents. "You're right," he sighed at last. "Let's eat and forget about it. No sense preparing for the worst when hopefully it will never happen. Let's count on the best and then work to make sure that it's a self-fulfilling prophecy."

By mutual agreement, they dropped the subject of Denis St. John, and Loralie managed to enjoy her fruit platter breakfast—fresh strawberries, honeydew melon, cantaloupe and kiwi fruit, along with a toasted English muffin and plenty of strong hot coffee.

Jon initialled the tab and charged it to his room number, then escorted Loralie outside onto Seventh Street.

The stroll was pleasant, the morning invigorating. Traffic crawled by on Seventh Street, preparing to turn the corner to head further uptown or across the river on the Martin Luther King, Jr. Bridge.

When they reached the building, the security officer looked at their badges and waved them inside. Members of the local coin show were already checking identities, signing in attenders, and issuing them name badges to wear into the bourse. The security officer was kept busy, directing throngs of people away from the doors and over to the side where the registration desk was.

"Sorry, no one allowed inside without signing

in and wearing a badge," he said.

Loralie appreciated the fact that the show's producers worked to create a safe environment, and she felt comforted to see the uniformed security personnel strategically located throughout the massive room.

There were tables laden with freebie copies of trade journals and tabloid publications to serve hobbyists. There were also stacks of convention brochures. Loralie retrieved a copy. A twenty-dollar gold piece, a St. Gaudens, was reproduced on the cover, where a paddle-wheeler steamboat sailed beneath the Arch that was positioned like a rainbow.

The brochure offered a wealth of information. Dealers were listed in alphabetical order, with their table assignments given, so that those attending could quickly locate friends by searching for a familiar name, jotting the number, then looking for spaces as one would in a mobile home park.

Loralie went to her table, whisked the covering away from the display cases, gave everything the once-over, then sat down to await potential customers. She noticed she wasn't the only dealer doing a noticeable lack of business, so she didn't feel too bad when the majority of the persons who came through the doors seemed to flock to the same groupings of booths again and again. She was glad, though, that Jon was obviously doing a thriving business, as was Christopher's, a jewelry wholesaler from Iowa, whose booth was close to hers.

She was not expecting it when Jon came to her table. "I left my assistant in charge. I thought I'd come by and table-sit your space for a little while so you can take a break."

"You're a dear. You're sure you don't mind?"

"Glad to do it. Who knows, maybe someday I'll badly need you to table-sit for me."

"I won't be long."

"No rush, Lor."

Loralie went to the rest rooms, then to the espresso stand for cups of coffee for the both of them. En route back, her eyes fell to several displays, and she saw items she needed to fill clients' want-lists.

"Have you made your way to any of the dealer tables yet?" Jon asked her when she returned to her booth.

"I haven't been able to. No assistant, remember?"

"I've done a lot of buying this morning. I've already spent almost ninety-thousand buying merchandise from other dealers. If you've got buying to do, Loralie, you'd better do it before other dealers beat you to it."

"I suppose I could cover up my display while I do. . . ."

"Nonsense!" Jon said. "I'll watch your table. My assistant isn't having any problem keeping up."

"Sell it all for me," Loralie teased, "so I can do lots of buying myself."

"I will," Jon said. "Write down your dealer code for me so I'll know what you paid for the items. That way I'll know how to set a fair price that allows you the right profit."

Loralie had never given out her dealer code before—letters representing specific numbers, written on the reverse of the coin holders to remind herself what she'd paid for an item. But somehow she trusted Jon, and she knew that with him there she would not risk losing her confidentiality.

"Go enjoy the bourse, Loralie. And good luck. Don't worry. Your business is in good hands."

"I know it is," she said sincerely. "The best."

As she made her way around the room, taking more time than she really wanted to, she made some fantastic deals. She lingered a bit longer than she'd planned because she wasn't sure if she'd get the opportunity again.

"Well, well, well! If it isn't Miss Southern Spitfire!"

Loralie winced.

There was a heavy thud as Denis St. John dropped a briefcase on what was obviously his table. With an impatient snap of his wrists, he flicked the ornate covering from his display. The case held extremely expensive coins, and some pre-owned diamond rings, both men's and women's, as well as antique jewelry. But what seemed most impressive were the stacks and stacks of pristine, newly released books *THE COMPLETE GUIDE TO COUNTERFEIT COIN DETECTION*—authored by none other than Denis St. John.

Loralie picked up a hardcover copy, rife with expensive illustrations. She looked at the front cover, then the spine, then flipped open the book to search for the printed price.

Even though the man had been nothing short of obnoxious to her, she remembered that a kind word could turn away wrath. She didn't intend to act like a doormat, but neither did she wish to continue in the role of adversary that it seemed Denis St. John had cast her. Perhaps it would smooth the troubled waters if she'd purchase one of his books, which she genuinely desired to own.

She'd been going to tease that she was his first customer, and might become his number one fan. But as soon as the man was seated and obviously open for business, dealers left their tables and thronged to his booth as if they were paying homage to the reigning king of numismatics. Loralie quietly hugged her copy of the book as she waited her turn.

Her turn did not come quickly, for Denis St. John wrote lengthy, intimate, and flowery inscriptions in each book he sold, even when the buyer was someone whose acquaintance he was making for the first time.

"I'd like a copy of your book for myself,"

Loralie said at last. Then on impulse she reached for another. "And please autograph one to Jonathan," she added. "He's been so wonderful to me that I'd like to give him a token of appreciation for his kindness. I know he would cherish your new book."

"Very well," Denis St. John said, his tone carefully indifferent, as if Loralie had no significance to him.

This time he did not take long. To Jon he wrote an inscription that was obviously loaded with inside jokes. To Loralie he wrote his name only and closed the book with an almost rude snap. "There you go."

Loralie handed him the money. "Keep the change," she murmured. She hadn't meant her words as an insult—but that's how Denis St. John took them. "Don't patronize me, you little Southern Snip! I could buy and sell you a dozen times over. Twenty times over. Probably *one hundred times over*."

Loralie felt her temper flare. She knew she had to get away, escape to her own table, before her anger and hurt could get the best of her and she'd end up responding in kind, and embarrassing herself in front of Jon and his friends, thereby ruining their initial good impression of her.

When she kept walking, silence enveloped the immediate area. She heard fumbling from Denis St. John's booth—then change was flung in her direction, plinking on the floor, and ricocheting off dealers' closed cases.

Loralie didn't know whether she wanted to laugh or cry. She did neither. Instead, she turned slowly, ignoring the money that had fallen on the floor at her feet.

"Denis St. John. . .don't be so petty and juvenile," she implored.

"Don't rile me," he said. "I'm warning you. Keep it up and you'll regret it. You haven't seen the last of me yet, baby. . . ."

Loralie held her head high as she returned to her booth several rows away from Denis St. John's space.

"Here's something for you," she told Jon. "A little token of appreciation, along with my thanks."

"Wow! Denny's new book. Hey, this is terrific—thank you! And will you look at that autograph? What a memory he has! I'd all but forgotten that funny encounter in Phoenix—"

Jon was staring at the book. But then his eyes were drawn to Loralie's face, which she kept down as she kept her fingers busy rearranging items on her table that were already in perfect order.

"What happened?"

"Nothing."

"Bearded the lion in his den, did you, and he roared at you?"

Loralie forced a smile over the imagery. "Something like that."

"If I didn't know better, Loralie dear, I'd think

that the inveterate bachelor, the not-the-marrying-kind Denis St. John is falling in love with you."

Loralie groaned. "Puh-leeze, Jon. Bite your tongue. Wash your mouth out with soap. Surely you jest."

"No, I'm more than a little serious. You're getting through to ol' Denny. Not very many women can, you know. Indifference is generally the armor he wears."

"Indifference? I can't even imagine it—but believe me, I think I'd prefer it to his...attentions, rude as they are. Why does he treat me the way he does?"

"I don't know. . . ."

"Yes, you do!" Loralie pressed on, sensing there was something Jon wasn't telling her. "Please care enough about me to be honest. I'm nothing to him. Why does he treat me the way he does?"

"I don't know for sure, mind you, but I have my suspicions."

"Do tell."

Jon checked his watch. "It's a long story. Can we postpone it until we dine tonight?"

"Curiosity is killing me. But the moment of truth will have to wait. Sure. And remember—this one's on me. You name the place."

Jon gave her a thick wad of cash and flipped her receipt book in her face, proof of what a busy man he'd been. His appearance in her booth had obviously drawn a lot of business she might not have warranted on her own.

"Whew!" she said, and gave a low, faltering whistle, the kind of whistle a man could probably have done unerringly. "When you choose a restaurant—hang the cost. My temporary assistant has earned the best."

"And the best is what we'll have. Even if we have to go a ways to get it," he added in a cryptic tone. "I think I know of just the place. I'll get back to you about it after I check something with a customer who was going to return after his college class today. I have something really special in mind," Jon promised.

With a warm heart, Loralie realized that "special" seemed true of every aspect of Jonathan McGuire's life. He was as kind, thoughtful, supportive, and inspiring in his personal dealings as he was in his professional. How Jon and Denny could be friends was almost beyond her, for two men couldn't have been more different. . . .

six

After Jon left there was a lull in business, then it picked up again, and for that Loralie was glad. As she made some sales and bought items off collectors with a desire to divest themselves of some duplicate material, her confidence soared.

She'd been aware that her morning's business had turned out well because Jon had been manning her booth. She'd been a bit unnerved, made afraid that left to her own devices and reputation she might have a slow day.

She noticed that the longer she transacted business, more people stopped at her booth because others were there. And once there, to her delight, many of them found items that they couldn't resist acquiring.

She passed out business cards, radiated southern hospitality, and she felt that she'd done a lot to pave the way for solid relationships with some midwestern collectors and the coterie of dealers as well.

She was almost welcoming it when the crowds thinned. Jon came by long enough for her to take a relief break, get another cup of coffee, then return to man her own table.

It felt good to sit down and take a breather. She reached for the gold show brochure, planning on reading it more carefully. Soon she was immersed in the information, her attention riveted to the page that was brimming with information about the Cervantes Convention Center and surrounding area.

By the time Loralie had read inward several pages beyond the 'Welcome' page, she'd learned that the Alfonso J. Cervantes Convention and Exhibition Center opened in 1977. It was referred to locally as "The Convention Center," "The Cervantes," "The Center," and "The Civic Center." Regardless of how people referred to it, the universal recognition was that it played a special role in the city that hugged the shoreline of the Mississippi River and sprawled inward, running north and south long distances from the Poplar Street and MLK Bridges.

The Cervantes Convention Center had impressed Loralie when she'd had her first view of it, but she realized there was a lot that had not yet met her eyes.

The City of St. Louis had spent years researching the pros and cons of America's great convention centers. When they had reached a decision to go ahead, they commissioned three world famous architectural and engineering firms to design the convention center.

The thirty-six-million-dollar center occupied a full four city blocks, and was in the midst of a sixteen block region that comprised the Convention Plaza Redevelopment Area.

Nearby were hotels, shops, restaurants, entertainment facilities, parking garages, and houses of worship. All that the city had to offer out-of-town guests, and local residents, too, was beneath the shadow of the towering Gateway Arch.

"Hi!" a young man said, interrupting Loralie's reading. "Are you Loralie Morgan?"

"Speaking," she said, smiling, as she arose to her feet. "What can I do for you?"

"My name is Gary Stanley. And Mr. McGuire—Jonathan—told me that you had some Standing Liberty Quarters, some common dates, but in high grade. I don't have an extensive collection, but I want to stick to high grade material for aesthetic reasons as well as investment stategy."

"That I do," she said, reaching for the appropriate box. She flipped through the coins that were in two-by-twos and flips, snugged in boxes as tightly as folders in a filing cabinet. She extracted half a dozen in varying grades, dates, and prices.

"These are *nice*," the young man said. "They'd really look good in my coin albums. . . ."

Slowly, almost reverently, the young man produced a quality magnifying glass and squinted through it, moving the glass slightly as he examined the coins.

"How much?" Gary inquired. "Price them together, and individually if you would."

"Sure thing," Loralie said.

She checked her code on the back, discounted a bit more when she learned the young man was a student at Southern Illinois School of Nursing in nearby Edwardsville, Illinois, and then quoted him the range of prices that he'd requested.

"I'll take this one for sure. I'll have to think about the others. I'd really like to—but I'm a little short."

"I know what that's like," Loralie said, smiling.

She could remember the days when paying ten dollars for a coin had seemed like an awful lot, too.

"Will you be here tomorrow?" he asked.

"Sure thing," Loralie said. "I'm here for the full run of the show."

"Great!" Gary said. "I have to work tonight. Maybe if it's a good shift I'll have the money and can come back tomorrow."

"I could set the coin back in case."

"You wouldn't mind?"

"Of course not. I'll set it back today, hold it tomorrow, and if you make it back, fine. If you're not able to, I'll put it back in inventory."

"I appreciate it, Ma'am. Mr. McGuire told me I'd enjoy doing business with you—and he's right."

"Well, you know how it is, Gary," Loralie said. "I appreciate the kind words. I always feel—if you don't like something—tell me. And if you like something—tell all of your friends."

"Right on!" Gary Stanley agreed.

Loralie felt herself stiffen when, as she was returning Gary's change to him and watching him pocket his purchase, Denis St. John was two tables away from hers.

Gary lingered, chitchatting a moment after their transaction, and for that Loralie was glad. She hoped that Denis St. John would bypass her table, treating her with a desired indifference. But it was not to be.

He gave Gary Stanley a curt nod, then without so much as a by-your-leave, he seated himself at Loralie's table and scrutinized her offerings through the glass. She felt almost as if he were appraising her, instead of her coins, and determined that both had been found wanting.

"Let me see that one," he said, and jabbed a fingertip at the glass case top, smudging the surface that Loralie had worked to keep print-free.

"Of course," she said, and obliged.

Gary seemed to sense the currents passing between them, and perhaps he saw he gratitude in Loralie's eye, for he hung around a bit longer than she believed he'd planned.

Denis St. John studied the coin a long, long time, then he reluctantly handed the coin back with an undecipherable grunt.

"Now let me see that one—"

And so it went on and on and on.

Loralie knew that Denis St. John wasn't in the market to buy coins, so she could only wonder what his intent was.

When her eyes fell on the cover of his book that was resting on the tabletop near the brochure, her heart skipped a beat. The king of counterfeit coin detection was obviously scouring her merchandise in hopes of publicly labeling her a fraud.

No sooner had the thought zinged into her mind than it happened in reality.

Denis arose, towering over her. He dropped the coin to the glass-topped case with disdain. "I'd pull that one if I were you," he said, his tone carrying to the next two tables in either direction. "It's a fake. You've got counterfeit material here."

Loralie felt her face flame.

She wanted to fall through the floor and have it miraculously close over her, never to be seen again, as dealers nearby looked at her with a new light of suspicion in their eyes.

"Are you sure?"

Denis gave a reckless laugh. "I wrote the book, didn't I?" he inquired.

"Yes, you did, and that's why I bought the book. To benefit from your widely respected wisdom. I'm afraid that I bought this piece in good faith. I hadn't taken time to send it in to ANACS for authentication and certification. I can't with all coins. . . ."

"Check page one hundred and twenty-five. Study it closely and perhaps you'll discover what reveals this coin to be a fake. There are generally things that give . . .all frauds. . .away."

His words were careful, controlled, seemingly innocuous to those nearby who were listening. But to Loralie they were like a direct slap in the face, for he'd as good as called her a fraudulent imposter before her peers who were close by.

Suddenly, Jonathan, who must've glanced in her direction, approached her table, casually, as if it was just happenstance. But Loralie knew better. She realized he'd discerned that there was trouble brewing.

"What seems to be the problem?"

"This. . .dealer. . .is offering fake gold."

"Really?"

Jonathan picked it up, reaching for his magnifying glass as he did so. "Wow. . .this is excellent, isn't it? A fake—but I'll wager that this one would've fooled ninety percent of the dealers in this room. Before I took your course at the ANA headquarters in Colorado, Denny, I'd have been suckered by this coin. I'd have bought it—and asked the guy for more."

Those at adjoining tables came to look. One by one they shook their heads, agreed that they, too, would have been fooled, and that after buying such a magnificent coin, would have trustingly offered it to their customers, believing it genuine.

"I've bought Mr. St. Denis' book, and he graciously autographed it, too," Loralie said to the dealers who milled around. "I trust that it'll educate me so I don't make a mistake like this again. I can highly recommend it to you. He has copies at his booth several rows over. As you've just seen, his knowledge in the field is second to none."

Denis seemed startled when Loralie was speaking up on his behalf, promoting his interests when he'd tried to publicly tear down her reputation, and cast allegations that she was a cheat and a sneak and a dishonest dealer intent on hoodwinking the buying public.

"Get back to your booth, Denny," a dealer said in a hearty tone. "I'd better get one of those books your little lady friend dealer is bragging about. Knowing you the book is probably overgraded and overpriced," the dealer teasingly ragged him. "But if it spares me from investing in just one counterfeit coin, it'll probably save me its price several times over. I want my copy autographed, too. And make sure what you write is fit for the wife and kids to see, you rascal, you!" he warned.

It was with relief that Loralie watched him walk away.

Gary Stanley was the last one to depart from her booth. "Well, I've got to get to work," he said. "It's been interesting. And I've enjoyed meeting you. I hope to see you tomorrow, Ma'am, if not before."

"Great. I'm looking forward to it, Gary."

When the scheduled day's events ended, Loralie was ready for a break.

"Tuckered out?" Jon asked when he arrived at her table as his assistant was closing up.

"Bushed," she admitted. "It's been a loooooonnnng day."

Jon shrugged. "You're a tenderfoot. You'll get toughened into it. A few months of doing this, and you'll find out that you thrive in such a pressure cooker environment."

"That's good to know."

"Hungry?"

"Famished."

"I know just the place. I've made arrangements to rent a car and take us there."

"Rent a car? How far is it? St. Louis has a lot of cabs."

"It's across the river. In Illinois. There's a place on Buchanan Street in Edwardsville. It's known for steaks. And the prices are unbelievable."

"Edwardsville? I met a nursing student today who was going to school at SIU-E."

"Gary Stanley?"

"As a matter of fact, yes."

"He's the one who recommended the place to me. That's where he works. He's a waiter. I promised we'd be seated in his station."

"How neat," Loralie said, laughing. "Now I know why he had a twinkle in his eyes when he told me that he'd see me tomorrow, if not before. You conspirators!"

"Guilty as accused," Jon said, grinning.

"Sounds great. But remember: this one's on me."

"Okay. Equal rights and equal *paying* if you insist."

"Which I do. . .tip included."

"The car's on me," Jon stipulated.

"Agreed," Loralie said, as she quickly retrieved the coin that she'd stored away for safekeeping in order for Gary to have a chance to return and claim it for his own. She knew exactly what she'd leave on the table for his tip! She smiled when she could envision the look of delight on his face. It was worth a bit more than a standard gratuity. But Loralie knew how much it would mean to him—perhaps more because she'd gifted him with it for service that she knew would be exemplary.

Jon and Loralie strolled back to the hotel, went to their rooms to freshen up, with Jon to come to her quarters when he was ready to depart.

She was slipping into her coat when he knocked. She checked the peephole then let him in.

"Just let me get my purse, spritz on a bit of perfume, and I'll be ready to go."

They were exiting Loralie's room when the

elevator doors yawned open. Denis St. John stepped out. He saw them closing the door to Loralie's room.

"Well, well, isn't this cozy?" he inquired in a droll tone. But his eyes looked oddly hurt—betrayed, even—which further puzzled Loralie.

"Don't say something you—we—will both regret," Jon warned carefully. "You know my reputation. And while you don't know Loralie's, you should be careful not to risk jeopardizing it by a form of false witness. We're off to dinner, and we'd love to have you join us, but we've got reservations for only two at an exclusive little club over in Illinois."

"Some other time," Denis said, and seemed oddly deflated.

"Yeah. Some other time," Jon said. "Soon. I'd like to see you two bury the hatchet. I like you both—and you're giving me a lot of undesired and undeserved stress the way you're carrying on. Especially you, Denny."

"Now you'd better watch what *you're* saying," Denis warned in a grim tone.

Without waiting for a reply, he slammed into his room which was just across the hall from Loralie's quarters.

"He's a complex and complicated man, isn't he?"

"And a haunted one, as well," Jon said.

"You're going to tell me about him?"

"It was a promise given. So yes. . .even though I doubt that Denis St. John would approve or appreciate. But then he seems to approve of and appreciate very little in life."

"He's a tortured individual, isn't he?"

"Very much so. He torments other individuals, as you've found out firsthand. But the person he tortures the most is himself. He's rigid toward others. Alas, he's truly unforgiving toward himself ....And because he is unable to forgive himself, he resists belief in the redeeming, saving grace of God ...."

"He's really to be pitied, isn't he?"

"Probably. Although if he realized people sometimes pity him, he'd be infuriated. Sometimes I think Denis purposely is boorish and difficult—so that he drives people away from him. He can't bear to be easily liked and accepted. Not when he can drive people away so that their alienation serves as a special form of self-inflicted punishment."

"He's really exemplary at all he does, isn't he?" Loralie's thoughts played over his accomplishments. "He gives his all to everything—good and bad. When he chooses to turn potential friends into enemies, he does it with the wit and wiles of a Grand Master. Just think of the good things that would result if he'd rechannel those efforts into serving the Lord."

"I pray—and have been praying—that one day that will happen. And it can happen someday, if God is willing, and if Denis St. John is humbled and frightened to the point where he realizes that he has no resources of his own upon which to call. And if he's made to understand that no matter what he owns, it's all without value if he has no personal relationship with the Lord."

A strange swell of emotions enveloped Loralie. Was that why she and Denis had mixed like oil and water? Was that why there was a chemistry that brought them quickly to the point of explosion? Was that why, when they came into contact, sparks flew? Was it because *she* was the one chosen by the Lord to bring him into the Christian fold?

At the thought she felt both faint-hearted with sudden romantic notions, even as she felt almost as weak with unmitigated fear.

She realized that deep down, the way he'd hurt, insulted, and lambasted her, she really didn't want anything more to do with him, personally or professionally.

But her wants were not what mattered. What was important was his salvation and relationship with a personal God. If she was the one used to help him to know the Lord, then she would willingly serve in any way that her Lord God so chose.

"Thy will, not mine," she murmured under her breath as Jon escorted her into Panatelli's Steak House where a smiling Gary Stanley stood ready to serve.

seven

When Loralie and Jon were seated, Gary arrived with glasses of ice water and their menus.

"What do you suggest?" Jon inquired of him.

The young waiter grinned, seeming proud of his hobby friends who'd driven twenty miles to visit his place of employment and sample the culinary specialties.

"We're known for our steaks," he said, pointing to a menu.

"Sounds good to me," Jon said.

He glanced across at Loralie, who realized she was famished enough to do justice to the large steak served with a salad, baked potato, and the restaurant's special sauce.

"I'll take that," Jon decided. "French dressing on the salad. The steak medium rare."

"Make it unanimous," she decided. "Blue cheese dressing. And my steak well done."

Gary nodded as he made the notations on his order pad.

"Coffee, black, for me," Jon said. "Lor?"

"Coffee—with cream," she decided.

"I'll be back with your dinner salads," Gary said as he departed with their order.

"He seems like a really nice fellow. I like him.

He reminds me of an associate back in Georgia. They're about the same age. But Jaydee's interest level in numismatics is even higher. He's in college studying engineering. I think the coin world is his true love, however."

"Will you take him into your business?" Jon asked.

Loralie frowned. It was a question she'd fielded many times, one she'd often asked herself. As her business expanded, she knew she'd have to trust key people to assist her and act on her behalf. But she wasn't sure Jaydee was the right one.

"I haven't made up my mind," she admitted. "He's a pleasant young man, and highly intelligent." She gave a light laugh. "I'm afraid he's one of those genius types who is so intelligent he has trouble tying his own shoelaces."

"I know the type. They can be brilliant with coins, especially doing the kind of work that Denis does in the field. But sometimes they're found wanting in the area of customer service."

"Exactly," said Loralie, realizing that Jon, sight unseen, had rather accurately summed up her young associate. She realized she didn't want to discuss her business, and the mention of Denis seemed a perfect way to move into that sensitive territory.

Just then Gary arrived with their dinner salads and the basket of assorted crackers.

"Ummmm. . .good!" Loralie said as she sampled a bite of salad.

"You'll probably find no finer in the city of Boston—"

"Or in Atlanta proper," Loralie agreed. She paused a moment and took a sip of her coffee. "You told me that you were going to tell me Denis St. John's story."

"That I did. Well, the topic that we were just on seems to lead into it quite nicely, actually," Jon said in a reflective tone. "Denny's father was in the coin business, and his mother was an heiress. They were people of wealth sufficient for Mrs. St. John to be able to offer her services on behalf of many charitable organizations. She also served as a 'table sitter' for her husband. Due to her interests and his, the St. Johns traveled a great deal."

"I see."

"Growing up, Denny went to shows when his schedule allowed—that was mainly summers and during school breaks. He went to military academies. The best that money could buy."

"That explains a lot," Loralie said. It seemed to give reason for his perfect posture, meticulous grooming, and his flawless manners—*when* he chose to use them. And it also seemed to offer a hint to his rigidity, and his attitude that he expected to be obeyed instantly when he issued either a request or a command.

"When Denny graduated from high school, quite naturally he was accepted by several of the finest Eastern colleges. He was lucky—he could choose among the colleges—Yale, Harvard,

Princeton. Most young men consider themselves lucky if they even get accepted by their least favorite choice."

"So I've heard."

"Denny went to college, taking up a study of business. He went through the years in record time, carrying a heavy credit load. He was younger than most when he graduated with his MBA. And at the same time, he was working to get his pilot's license, as well as assisting his father in the numismatics business."

"He must've been very, very busy."

"Denny's a workaholic. It's how he coped— then—and now."

"I've read articles about workaholism. My understanding is that although there is nothing illegal about it, and that in fact it is viewed by many as an admirable quality, in truth work can become like a 'drug of choice' so that labors numb an individual against things they can't face."

"Right. And then the result of all that effort brings feelings of self-esteem to the overachieving workaholic because she or he gets a sensation of validation from all of that production. Many people become workaholics because they *like* to work and find it satisfying, especially compared to the boredom of being comparatively idle. But there comes a time when anyone can cross the line that divides healthy attitudes toward work from compulsive ones. When no matter how much is accomplished...it's never enough. I think Denny's been there for quite a while now. ..."

"You think he's running from things? Using work to blot out things he'd rather not face? To keep at bay emotions he'd rather not feel?"

"That's exactly what I think."

"What's happened to him?"

"You name it, and he's probably suffered it. The man's had a lot of disappointments in life, and pain. He adored his parents. And his father was one of the most respected men in the hobby world. His mother, bless her heart, was adored by everyone. Wealthy as she was, she was generous almost to a fault. She never saw people as social classes. The poorest person on the street was an equal in her eyes."

"She sounds like a wonderful woman."

"She was. Our parents used to socialize when our mothers would be 'table-sitting' at bourses over the years. They'd go out for dinner in the evenings and perhaps take in entertainment. That's how Denny and I first met—accompanying our families."

"You have a long history, then."

Jon nodded. "I feel I know him as well as anyone—better than most."

"What happened to his parents?"

"They were fishing off Nantucket on a vacation holiday. They were lost at sea. Their bodies were never found."

"How awful. ..not to even be able to bury your

parents."

"It was bad. There was no doubt in anyone's mind that the St. Johns had drowned, for their boat was found, capsized, with flotsam in the area. But Denny refused to believe it. He's such a survivor that death is something he finds . . .rather inconceivable. He certainly doesn't acknowledge death as the natural conclusion to a life on this earth. And he certainly doesn't view bodily death as the gateway to eternal life. He considers death an affront and an insult to his human powers."

"He's not alone there. Many people share his views."

"The St. Johns' attorneys handled the settling of the estate. At age twenty-five, Denny St. John found himself a fabulously wealthy young man, for he had inherited his father's coin business, lock, stock, and display cases. Plus, he'd also been bequeathed his mother's wealth and her trust funds and annuities, which resulted in handsome earnings every year."

"At least he didn't have to know what it was to want. Not all orphans have that option," Loralie said.

"Denny's holdings were what kept him going. He threw himself into the coin business, and he began to travel extensively. There were times when I felt almost as if he were. . .running from himself, hopping on flight after flight in order to try to escape his pain. As if, if he hurried enough to catch a new plane he could leave himself and his unaddressed fears and concerns on the earlier flight, and feel free at last."

"I thought he flew to shows himself."

"That came a bit later. He would rent airplanes sometimes when the show schedules were tight and the arrangements to get from one to the next became a bit convoluted. As his show attendance became more compulsive, and his workaholism deepened, yes, he bought his own aircraft so that he could shave required travel time off his schedules."

"He's not a patient man. I can just imagine what he was like if a flight was canceled, or delayed, or if, heaven forbid, the airline had overbooked and he got bumped."

"I have seen it. And it was not a pretty sight."

"As busy as he was with shows, and as large as the St. John holdings are, he must've had really great help back at the shop."

"He did," Jon said. "The late Martin St. John's employees loved him dearly. Marty was as laid back and congenial as Denny can be overbearing and abrasive. Martin was prepared to listen to reason and make allowances for the human condition. Denny gave one hundred and ten percent of himself—and he expected no less of his employees."

"I'll bet he could be a real bear to work for. Especially if something beyond his control went wrong."

"That's exactly what the firm's employees began to conclude. They stayed on quite a while out of Martin's memory. But eventually, because they were such good people in the field, offers came in. One by one they left for greener and more peaceful pastures, so to speak. With each employee who severed himself from the St. John firm, Denny took it as a personal betrayal. I'm sure it hurt his self-esteem. He felt rejected. What he couldn't seem to realize was that he was not his father's son in certain ways."

"So what did he do?"

"He felt that other people had raided his work force—so he went to bourses, looked for good, key people employed with other firms. And he bought them. He made them offers that they couldn't refuse. Granted, he paid them very, very well. But in return he came to feel he owned them body and soul. A few have been with him many years. I feel most of them overlook a lot because, like me, they know that while to the world he appears to 'have it all,' in actuality he's a haunted, troubled, hurting, and deeply unhappy man."

"He never had time to have a relationship with a woman? To marry?"

"Actually, yes, he did have a relationship. But he approached that as he did so many other things. When he was busy raiding other numismatic corporations' employee lists, he met a young woman—Ciera Comstock."

"Pretty name."

"And fitting a very pretty woman. Denis St. John comes from a long line of distinguished people, and rumor had it that Ciera Comstock was an heiress. She certainly had the looks and behavior to suggest she was a debutante."

"It was love at first sight?"

"No," Jon said, smiling. "Business was always first and foremost in Denny's mind. He probably didn't even really see Ciera as a romantic possibility. He hired her for her book-keeping abilities, and her computer capacities, with the belief that with state-of-the-art programs and methods she could maintain an up-to-the-minute inventory. That way Denny could use electronic marketing methods and buy a coin one minute and sell it at a handsome profit five minutes later."

"Many big dealers have used those methods very successfully."

"True. *We* at McGuire Coin Gallery make use of the latest technology, purchasing updated equipment as soon as it's available."

"You make my methods feel positively prehistoric," Loralie said.

"Don't feel bad."

"To ever switch over from my current methods, I'd have to find my own Ciera Comstock. So I can understand Denis' need."

"Pretty soon Ciera was an established part of Denny's coterie. She accompanied him to shows. But she was no table sitter. She knew the business as well—some said *better*—than he. She wasn't content to sit on the sidelines and knit or read as many coin dealers' wives or girlfriends do. She got right out there and mixed and wheeled and dealed herself."

"Denis must have been impressed with her."

"Decidedly so. Proud as punch, he was. I guess he felt as if he'd 'created' her. Served as sort of a numismatical Henry Higgins, with Ciera Comstock his coin-associated Eliza Doolittle. Denny had complete trust in her. Ciera's word was as good as his and the dealers knew it. She was empowered to write checks. You name it, Denny gave her authorization."

"Somehow, I can't imagine him trusting anyone like that."

"Trust me, he did. And it was Ciera Comstock who taught him not to trust, to expect betrayal from one and all."

"What happened?"

"Ciera made herself invaluable to him. And she tantalized him with her mystique. She was a mysterious woman. She could be friendly, but no one was allowed inside to where she kept her own thoughts and counsel, behind that practiced, artful, socially correct debutante's smile."

"Was she pretty?"

"Very. You look very much like her. In fact, I think that's one reason why Denny's taken on so in your direction. Your hair's about the same color. You're about the same height and size. Her eyes were hazel, while yours are brown. But there are certain resemblances in bearing, et cetera. I think, without his awareness that it's happening, the sight of you has sparked within Denny a lot of feelings he didn't deal with long ago. And doesn't want to deal with now. Your presence sort of . . .goads. . .him into facing things. . .and he doesn't like it."

"It's not my fault I resemble a woman once important to him, by whom he feels betrayed."

"Of course not. Logically, we can see that. But in his hurt and pain, sometimes Denny St. John is impulsive rather than logical."

"What happened between Ciera and Denny?"

"She made herself indispensable to him. To the point where I don't think he believed he could live and function without her. She'd stepped into his life when it was rather chaotic, and brought order into his universe. Her behavior was always flawless. If Denny was being a bit harsh—Ciera would step in and smooth the situation. She was worth her weight in gold to him. And he knew it. Several years ago on her birthday he gave her a five carat diamond ring."

"Whew! I've never even *seen* a diamond that big. And at coin shows I've seen some impressive gems."

"It was the talk of the industry when Denny announced their engagement. Ciera played the role of the blushing, happy bride-to-be. But that mask quickly fell from place to be replaced by her tough businesswoman attitudes. She'd invested a

lot of efforts in Denny's family business—
although I know she was well paid. But seeing
herself as the future Mrs. Denis St. John, she
began to want more. Denny was so captivated by
her—and so grateful—that he let her have it. He
would have given her the moon and stars had it
been in his power. And she would have accepted
them—and sweetly demanded more. She was
nothing more than a bejeweled, beautifully
coiffed, designer label-clothed, gold-digging little guttersnipe."

"Oh, Jon!" Loralie had not heard him talk
harshly about anyone, and she knew for him to
label Ciera Comstock with such uncharitable
words meant that the unvarnished truth was
probably even worse. "Did he finally see her for
what she was? Did she break his heart?"

"I don't think Denny St. John ever antes up his
heart in any kind of dealings, business or pleasure. But if he offered even a part of himself—she
probably broke his heart. What she tried to do was
to 'break the bank.'"

"How was she going to do that?"

"With computer technology. Some think that
Denis St. John is a genius. There were as many
who felt that Ciera Comstock was a genius in her
own perverse way, too. When it came to book-
keeping and electronic ledgers, money transfers,
and such things, the woman was brilliant. She
could make the numbers walk and talk—and tell
lies. The way she was juggling money around,

she could've been employed by a circus. She was keeping money kiting around among accounts with sleight-of-electronic tricks so that Denny was unaware she was raiding various accounts and preparing to make huge electronic transfers to an account she'd set up in Switzerland."

"How awful!"

"Greed is an interesting thing, you know. Most people fail in their deceitful behaviors because they get *too* greedy. And so it was for Ciera. She wasn't content to take the bulk of Denny's liquid and easily liquidated holdings. She wanted it *all*. That required time. She gambled against the clock—and lost."

"Thank goodness!"

"She had her ducks all in a row. She was ready to make her moves, indeed, she'd begun them. But a minor employee at one of the banks caught a discrepancy, and knowing that Denny St. John took care of people who were loyal to him, this fledgling employee, perhaps hoping to be kindly remembered if Denny was ever in a position to do a favor, gave him a call. Denny flew home—unexpectedly. He went straight to the shop. Just as he was approaching—he saw a long, black Mercedes parked in front, the trunk open. He slammed on the brakes, watched, and he saw Ciera, who was dressed as if she expected to travel, get into the car after stowing several of his coin cases in the trunk."

"She was robbing him of his inventory?"

"Yes. And he noticed that when she got into the car—she didn't even turn around and lock the front doors to his establishment. Neither did Denny. I guess he preferred to take his chances with the basically honest man-on-the-street, rather than risk losing sight of the woman who had stolen his heart and then set out to strip him of the business interests amassed by his family over the generations."

"What happened?"

"It was like something out of a television police show. There was a high speed chase. Denny is a good driver. In high school he'd raced stock cars. He can handle himself whether it's in a plane, a car, or a bicycle. . . . He outdrove and outmaneuvered the getaway car. The Mercedes slammed into a bridge abutment. The driver was killed instantly. His head went through the windshield. He wasn't wearing a seat belt."

"And Ciera?"

"She lived for two hours. Denny was devastated. I think he actually had cared about her, more than he'd ever cared about anyone except his mother and father. He couldn't believe she'd betrayed him. Didn't want to believe it. But she had. She'd laid the plans with premeditated calm, executing the smallest details with dispatch. She and her accomplice had set it up to look as if she'd been kidnapped. They had their passports and airline tickets—with the schedules down to the minute. They had a portable laptop computer, and from the airport, she was going to dial back to the shop and use the computer capacities to have one computer use telephone lines to transmit directions to the other. And on the computer in Denny's office was a program file just waiting to execute the complicated commands that would electronically transfer his funds, his life's earnings, into Ciera Comstock's accounts in Switzerland. Where Denny couldn't touch the money— even though it was rightfully his.''

"How awful."

"Denny was numb. He was at the hospital as Ciera lay dying, barely conscious. She'd meant so much to him and she lay near death. A nurse I know who was there said that even after what Ciera had done to him...Denny looked at her with love...and spoke of love. Even forgiveness."

"How poignant. There must be a nicer side to him after all."

"With her dying breath, Ciera looked at him with scorn and hate in her eyes, though they were swollen almost shut from the head injuries. She said, 'You fool! I never loved you! And I'd never have married you... I'm already married...to the man who was with me.' And then when she realized her husband had died in the accident, she began to cry."

"What a blow that must've been."

"The biggest blow was to Denny's ego. He thought Ciera had cared about him, and what he learned minutes before she passed away is that she had purposely set about to fall in with him, to be asked into his employ. They'd selected him as ripe for the plucking and then executed the necessary steps to make it happen."

"What a cold and calculated woman," Loralie said.

"Agreed. So Denny's never loved again. Never. Now he won't even try. It seems impossible for him to trust. He thinks all women are calculated, conniving, cold-hearted, deceitful lying creations."

"I don't agree with him, but I can understand why he feels that way."

"Denny is awful to you, Loralie, and I realize that. So do the other dealers. Especially those who are privy to his sad story. But try not to hate him. He's to be pitied—and to be prayed for—if you can and will."

"As a Christian, I consider it a duty. . .and an honor. I would like for such a hurt, angry, sad human being, whether a wealthy man like Denis St. John, or the poorest homeless individual on the street, to know the healing power of God's love and caring."

"I thought so, and that's why I've taken you into my confidence, so that you can want the best for Denis St. John, even when he angrily resists accepting the Lord and all that He has to offer."

"Which can never be taken away. Or transferred to another's account in Switzerland. . . ."

Jon smiled when he saw Gary approaching with

a heavily laden tray. "It appears our timing is right. The business is out of the way, the food's arrived, so the rest of the night can be spent in pleasurable conversation."

After they had eaten, Loralie waited for her charge card and the bill to be brought back for her signature. "The food was as delicious as Gary assured you it would be," she said. The gratuity had been included in the bill, but she said nothing about her own planned additional tip in thanks for Gary helping them to have such an enjoyable evening.

"Ready to go?" Jon asked, helping her with her coat.

"Uh-huh." She slid her hand into her coat pocket, and surreptitiously slid the coin to the table. It was enclosed in a two-by-two with Gary's name written on it so that no one would think it had been left by accident.

Jon, spotting the coin positioned by the candle arrangement, picked it up, curious.

"Forget something?" he asked. He flipped the container over and saw Gary's name imprinted.

Carefully he replaced it, grinning, for he knew what the coin would mean to the young man. And he realized that more than the value of it would be the sentiment sent along with it.

"He'll probably someday tell his grandchildren how this coin came into his possession. It'll be a keeper. One he never sells."

"And if he goes into the business—keeping that

will make him no less a true professional dealer, right?"

"Right. You know, Loralie Morgan, you are one very nice lady."

"Thank you."

"I think that deep down, Denny St. John believes so too, but it galls him to realize it, let alone consider admitting it."

"Until you told me his story, I felt he was thoroughly reprehensible. I was thinking about all kinds of things I'd like to see him give up for Lent!"

Jon laughed. "Sometimes you are incorrigible. A Christian with real spice and zest. Speaking of Lent—this Sunday is Palm Sunday. Are we on for attending worship services together?"

"I'd love that."

"If you don't mind, Loralie, I think I'll see if Denis wants to go, too."

"It doesn't hurt to ask," she agreed, even though deep in her heart she felt that donkeys would fly before the likes of Denis St. John would darken the doors of a church. At least not in *her* company.

"He's a very lonely man," Jon said. "As hurt by Ciera as he was, he tries to manipulate relationships so they're always on his terms."

"When we know those arranged by the Lord are the best."

"And the best is really what we'd both like Denis St. John to have."

eight

Loralie found herself relieved that Sunday was two days away. The idea of attending church with Denis St. John in tow unnerved her, but she realized that if he was present at the worship services, it would be because God intended for it to happen.

The following morning after a quick breakfast, Loralie and Jon exited the hotel onto Seventh Street and hastened to the entrance into the bourse area.

There were good crowds, as the weekend was upon them, and Loralie was pleased to be doing a brisk business. Buying, selling, buying more, selling more, and setting aside some new acquisitions to take back to Georgia to offer to her regular clientele at the shop.

Jon was a steadying influence during the course of the show. He, or his assistant, were wonderful about periodically coming to her booth so that she could take a break and get a cup of coffee or a sandwich from the concession stand. Even so, the days were long and grueling, and she realized she'd be glad when Sunday afternoon arrived and she could depart on the early evening flight that would take her home.

The show had been an unqualified success. As valuable as the sales she'd made and the purchases she'd acquired, had been the contacts she'd made through Jon. She now counted many key people among her hobby friends. She found herself looking forward to some of the upcoming scheduled shows, for she knew she would be seeing these individuals again there. She knew the day was coming when before she even left the Atlanta area, she'd have dinner dates booked for every night of the show as she'd relax and fellowship with new friends in the hobby.

Jon hadn't been booked ahead on this trip, although she was aware that he could have, and he'd been wonderful about squiring her around each evening. Her feelings toward him had subtly changed, however.

At first there had been some attraction, and she'd realized what a wonderful husband he'd make for some woman. She was aware that initially he'd been drawn to her in that way, too. But as their friendship developed, she realized they both were aware they'd rather remain deep and close friends than try for a relationship that probably wasn't meant to be.

Jon didn't make her pulse race. He didn't make her knees feel weak. He didn't fill her daydreams with sweet longings. He was like a rock to support her. A friend to be counted on. A business associate to guide her as a mentor. She realized that while he was a rare and precious find of a friend. . .he was not the right man for her. The man chosen by God.

What bothered her, however, was that all the things Jon failed to do to her pulse and thought processes—Denis St. John managed to accomplish—even against her will. She found herself thinking about him, even when she wanted not to. Although it caused her cheeks to heat with a blush, at times she imagined what it would be like to kiss him. And the one rare time when he'd actually *smiled* at her, it had set her heart to racing. Each time she recalled that pleasant and almost friendly interlude, her heart sped anew.

She found herself both anticipating—and dreading—Sunday morning. She anticipated attending church with Denis. At the same time she dreaded it. Then, to her consternation, she found herself also dreading the idea that he might refuse to attend.

"It's confusing, that's what it is," she muttered to herself.

She hadn't seen Denis St. John approach her table. "Classic next-to-the-last-day syndrome," he said, tsk-tsking with his tongue and teeth. "I've seen it before, many times."

"What are you talking about?" she asked, feeling a bit defensive, though she hoped the feeling wasn't apparent.

"Talking to yourself. That's what I'm talking about. It's a sign that it's time to empty the display cases, pack your bags, and head home to normalcy after the enjoyable insanity of a multi-day bourse."

"Ah. . .so that's what it is?"

"The diagnosis of an expert."

"How do you know that. . .I'm not. . .faking it?"

He gave her a look, one that she had a hard time understanding. Something shot through his eyes. She was unsure if it was pain, hurt, embarrassment. Not that it really mattered.

"I. . .think. . .you've learned your lesson about fakes. And," he paused, "perhaps I have, too."

What? Loralie thought. *That sounds amazingly like an apology, from a man I'd believed was constitutionally incapable of saying he's sorry.*

"We can hope so. For both of us," Loralie said to fill the silence that sprang between them.

Denis toyed with the edge of her table. He seemed somehow almost shy.

"Something I can help you with?"

"Well, yes. Tonight being Saturday night, I'm making reservations to take a group of dealer friends out. I-I'd like you to join us."

"Is Jon going?"

"Of course. He's one of my oldest and trusted friends."

"We're not Siamese twins for the duration of this show, Mr. St. John. Jon's a big boy. And I'm a big girl. I can take care of myself. You needn't invite me along like a fifth wheel."

"Jon wants you there. I want you there. And I know that the others will enjoy making your acquaintance."

"Let me think about it, okay?" Loralie said.

"What's to think about?" Denis asked, seeming dismayed and miffed that with the offer of his invitation there was not an immediate acceptance.

"I have this bad habit of trying to refrain from going where I'm not wanted," she replied softly.

"And I've done a commendable job of making you feel like *persona non grata*?"

"'Fraid so."

"Then let me make it up to you. Starting tonight."

"I'll let you know. Soon."

"I know how you feel, Loralie. I, too, try to make it a point not to go where I'm not wanted. Jon's been asking me to attend church with you both tomorrow. Like you, I told him that I'd have to let you know. And for the same insecure reason. . . ."

"But you're wanted, Denis," Loralie softly said. "The Lord wants you to come to His house of worship, so you can feel at home with Him. Get to know Him as others do, who consider Him their Best Friend in life. The Friend Who never fails them. The One who never betrays."

"That's what Jon said," Denis admitted in a voice scarcely above a whisper. "I know how you and Jon feel about your faith. I realize that Jon wants me at church services with him. And a part of me wants to go, for some unusual reason. But

I won't attend if I know that you really would prefer I not be there. One of the worst feelings in the world is to suffer the sensation of being an interloper. An unwanted guest."

Loralie saw her chance. "I'm a business-woman, if nothing else," she said, casually fluffing her hair as her pulse pounded. "So I'll strike a deal with you, Denis St. John. We both have been honest about our feelings of insecurity. So I tell you what—I will accept your invitation to dine with your party tonight, and accept it with pleasure, if you will accept our invitation to attend worship services in the morning."

Denis didn't take long to think it over. He extended his grip. "You've got a deal, buddy."

"Great. And, Denis, thanks for making me feel like 'one of the boys'. I appreciate it."

He looked her up and down. "Only figuratively, my dear. For no one could literally ever make that mistake."

"See you tonight," Loralie said.

"I'll have a limo outside the hotel. We'll be dining at the Boston Seafood Company. You like seafood?"

"Next to Georgia peaches—it's my favorite food!"

"It'll be a night to remember. Oh. . .and if you care to bring it along tonight, or produce it sometime tomorrow, Loralie, I'd really like to write a personal inscription in the book I autographed for you. Tonight will be special.

Memories will be made of it—so surely it'll give me something personal to inscribe."

"Tonight will be special," Loralie agreed. "And tomorrow, too. . . ."

Because Loralie and Jon had seen Gary Stanley at his place of employment at Edwardsville the night before, she really did not expect to see him on Saturday as he'd suggested might happen. She was surprised and delighted when he appeared at her booth. He hung around, visiting, and she discovered that she really liked the student nurse who was going to be graduating in December with his degree.

The Saturday afternoon crowds were busy, Loralie needed a break, and Jon and his assistant were busy at their table. When Gary continued to hang around, she inquired if he might be agreeable to watching her bourse table for a few minutes.

He gave a beaming grin. "I'd love to!" he said. Then he told her that it was his dream to one day be a part-time coin dealer, and when he retired from a nursing career to perhaps opt for a second full-time career as a dealer.

"Then get your feet wet now," Loralie teased.

She quickly explained the rudiments, then left him on his own. She didn't feel a need to rush because she had trust in the young man. She'd talked to him long enough to realize he was ethical, honest, and personable. In addition, his knowledge of numismatics was extensive, for he studied the publications and was amassing a personal library of reference books. Loralie felt warm feelings for the college student, almost like an older sister to him.

She saw that Denis wasn't busy at his booth, and searching for an excuse to stop by, she realized what a nice token of friendship and appreciation for his helping her it would be if she gifted Gary with an autographed copy of Denis' book.

"Hi—got another copy of your book I can buy?"

Denis St. John gave her an amused look. "You're selling almost as many for me as I am for myself. I got writer's cramp autographing all of them that sold as a result of your word-of-mouth recommendation after I suggested you not sell that 'bad' gold piece."

"This is for a young friend of Jon's and mine." Loralie nodded in the direction of her table. "He's been keeping me company this afternoon, and I pressed him into serving as a table-sitter for a little while so I could take a break. I thought I'd give him one of your books. He's serious about the hobby and studies zealously. He's a student nurse but wants to deal part-time, maybe choosing it for a secondary career. So your book would be valuable to him for many years."

Denis opened the flyleaf. "What's his name?"

"Gary. Gary Stanley."

"Okay."

Loralie watched as Denis wrote: "Best wishes, Gary Stanley. Any friend of Loralie and Jon's is a friend of mine. Denis St. John."

"He'll treasure this, I'm sure. Thanks."

"You're welcome. See you tonight. We'll meet in the lobby. Sevenish."

"I'm really looking forward to it."

"I think you'll enjoy the eclectic collection of dealers."

"Well, you know what they say: 'A stranger is a friend you simply haven't had a chance yet to meet.'"

Loralie felt a tingle of excitement when she approached her own table where Gary was expertly handling a customer, showing the man her wares, describing the important differences to keep in mind when comparing the coins of the same year and mint mark.

"Great job," she congratulated as she let him finish transacting the negotiation. "You're a natural at this, kid."

"I love doing it."

"It shows. By the way, I got a little something for you, Gary. Here."

She handed him the book, personally autographed to him, and she was gratified at how his eyes lit up. Joy radiated from his features. He seemed to savor every word of the inscription.

"Why don't you run over to Denis' booth and personally meet him?" Loralie said. "He's actually a very nice person," she smoothly assured, even though her initial experiences with the man had been anything but.

"You don't mind?"

"Of course not. But report back to me and let me know how it went."

"I sure will!"

Gary disappeared, and he was so long in returning that Loralie had begun to think maybe he'd been detained and then unable to return to her table to bid her goodbye. She was straightening her table and putting the stall in order when he returned. One look at him and she knew he was walking on air.

"Wow! He's every bit as nice as you said he was. We've shop-talked for what seemed like hours. He talked to me like I was an equal to him. And he gave me all kinds of advice. Then he asked me if I was free tonight. Loralie, he invited me out to have dinner with a group of his coin dealer friends."

"I hope that you accepted."

"Well...yeah, I finally did, although I felt kind of like I was imposing."

"Great, Gary, because Jon and I are both among those Denis is hosting for the evening."

"Neat! Now I know I'll feel more comfortable going along."

"I view it as not only a social event, but as a learning experience, too. I figure listening to the veterans in the field will teach me a lot about what

I yet have to learn."

"It'll be a night to remember," Gary mused. "This entire show has been a dream come true."

"For me, too, Gary, for me, too. And all because of people like Jon, Denis, and you. . . ."

nine

Loralie quickly showered, fixed her hair, reapplied makeup, then put on the dressiest outfit she'd brought to St. Louis.

She was ready promptly on time. Gary Stanley was just entering the lobby when she stepped off the elevators. She went to him and together they approached Jon and a group of dealers who were waiting for Denis St. John and the limousine to arrive.

"I'll do the introductions in Denis' stead since he's not here," Jonathan McGuire said.

"Loralie, this is Jim Beasley of Tilden Coins, Ford Hickey, next to him is Steve, President of Steve's Coins, and Wayne Haythorne, Jr., a very serious collector we've all enjoyed serving over the years. Steve and Wayne are the promoters and driving forces behind S & W Coin Auctions, of Effingham, Illinois, an emerging force in the field of estate dispersal of numismatic items, who sometimes schedule auctions for dealers as well. And of course you already know Gary Stanley, who's a senior at SIU-E School of Nursing in nearby Edwardsville, Illinois."

Everyone shook hands all the way around and when Denis arrived, they were ushered out to the stretch limo and taken to the Boston Seafood Company where a table was reserved for their dinner party. Loralie didn't know which was better, the food or the companionship, for both were excellent.

She and Gary, especially, enjoyed the riveting stories that the veteran dealers swapped. While the tales were amusing, they were also educational, and Loralie realized how hard-won was some of the knowledge that the dealers shared among friends. Warnings. Tips. Hints. Hot trends. Security measures to take.

"Denis, thank you so much for inviting me to dine as your guest this evening," Loralie said. "I really enjoyed it—and you—very much."

"A sentiment most sincerely returned. And, listen. . .I'm really sorry that you and I got off on the wrong foot a few days ago. I wasn't raised like that. I probably should've been taken out and horsewhipped for my ungentlemanly behavior."

"I had my moments of feeling like doing exactly that. . . ."

"And with good reason. I was goading you. But I'm really not like that at all."

"That's what Jon's been telling me."

"You and Jon really hit it off, didn't you?"

"I like him very much, yes."

She realized the area that Denis St. John was entering into, and she felt both trepidation and a sense of tantalization.

"But you two don't have any kind of. . .

understanding?"

"Oh, heavens, no. We're just friends."

Denis's face grew solemn. "Why I inquire is because tonight, being in your company on a casual basis, and seeing you interact with others—well, it made me realize I want to get to know you better. A lot better."

"We can start by seeing one another at church services in the morning."

Denis looked momentarily frustrated. "I meant beyond that."

"But I'll be flying out of Lambert Field tomorrow. An early evening flight. The first one scheduled for me to make after the bourse closes."

"It's not like you're going to the next planet. I do have a plane. And my life's my own."

"That sounds suspiciously like you're investigating if it's possible to see me on our own time, on my turf."

"I guess that's exactly what I'm asking. There's no boyfriend back in the Atlanta area who'd become upset if I appeared on-scene?"

"None. I've been too busy for a social life, I'm afraid."

"Maybe we can align our calendars and work out something in the near future. And if not, perhaps we'll run into each other at some upcoming show dates. We'll have to check our calendars to see when we'll be in the same place at the same time and then make a solid commitment to go out for dinner."

"I'd like that very much. Denis, in spite of how I've acted toward you, I do admire, respect, and like *you*."

"I know you do, Loralie. And that's what's so impressed me. I gave you myriad reasons to despise me. But you returned hatred with acceptance. I-I haven't had great successes lately with women. . . ." His voice broke off.

Loralie knew he was thinking of Ciera Comstock, as was she, although Denis was unaware that Jon McGuire had made her privy to his friend's personal heartbreak and disillusionment.

"I'm sorry. When we've been hurt in the past, it makes it harder to trust again. And then, too, pride can get in the way."

Denis lifted his eyes to hers. "You really do understand, don't you?"

She nodded. "More than you might ever realize."

"You're one in a million, Loralie. There's nothing false and phony about you. You're the genuine article. . . ."

"I'm only human, Denis. I have my flaws and failings, too. We all do. Only the Lord is the perfect example in living. The rest of us, no matter how hard we try, often fall short. But day by day I do the best I can."

"And you do an exemplary job."

"I'll see you in the morning for church."

"Okay. And I'll see you in the afternoon at the show. And tomorrow evening."

"But I'm leaving in the early evening hours."

"So am I. So I thought that we could share a cab to the airport, and then I'd see you off before I collect my Cessna and fly off into the wild blue yonder."

"That would be lovely, if you don't mind."

"I would mind terribly if you refused."

"Then I'll agree—with pleasure."

The following morning Jon, Denis, and she took a cab to a nearby church. The big city congregation was friendly. The pastor welcomed them, directed them to the guest registry, and the usher promptly seated them. The church was appealing and nicely decorated with floral tributes for the Palm Sunday services. The organist was excellent, and the custom-made pipe organ filled the massive stone and oak-beamed structure with uplifting music that encouraged the congregation to lift their voices in songs of praise.

Loralie knew some of the happiest moments of her life as she was seated between Jon, a friend so dear, and Denis St. John, a complicated fellow who'd made clear he wanted to get to know her much better. When Denis sang old favorite hymns selected for the service, and didn't have to consult the hymnbook and stumble through the lyrics, she realized he'd had some church background, even if he'd gotten away from it.

Then she remembered what Jon had told her about the late Mrs. St. John and it seemed natural that such a civic and charity-minded woman would probably have been active in church work, too.

During the services Loralie prayed that if Denis had wandered from the faith of his fathers, he would return to the fold. She suspected a love of God had been instilled in him before his hurt and heartache had driven him to rebellion—rebellion against both women and the God who created them.

The trio lingered for a moment outside on the wide church steps, then Jon hailed a taxi, and they piled in for the ride back to the Convention Center and an afternoon spent at the bourse.

Ordinarily Loralie did not do any work on Sundays. She reserved the day for church activities, pleasurable pursuits, and fellowship with close friends. The four-day convention was planned to include the Sabbath, though, and she'd signed an agreement promising to keep her booth open for the hobbyists. For them, Sunday afternoon was a day they and their families could attend a show catering to their pleasurable interests. The rare times Loralie was at a coin show on Sunday, she viewed it as service to others to help them with their leisure time activities.

Business was slow, which she did not mind, for she enjoyed relaxing herself and passing the time chatting with her new friends.

"Oh, Loralie!" a voice called out. "I'm so glad you haven't left for Atlanta already." She recognized Gary Stanley's youthful voice even before she turned to greet him.

"Hi, stranger!" She gestured for him to come behind her table where he could take a chair and visit with her.

"I'm like a bad penny," he said ruefully. "Always showing up again."

"Oh, you are not," she said, laying a friendly hand on his shoulder. "I've enjoyed our times together. I'm glad you made the effort to return."

"I wasn't doing anything special after church services, so I grabbed a 'burger at a fast-food joint—and here I am!"

"Ah...I think it's the budding future coin dealer in you, Gary, just straining to make an emergence now. You have it in your blood. You're hooked. You can't stay away!"

"Maybe it is," he agreed. "I do want to do this someday. You've been such an inspiration to me. You give me the encouragement to realize that I can do it—if I want to."

"Why, thank you!"

"I'm serious," he said. "So many of the dealers here have had families in the business for several generations. They walk into full blown and successful financial concerns. But you've really started the business you have from the ground up. Granted, you had some posthumous help from your father. But you're the driving force behind what you do."

"In many ways that's true. You can do it too, you know."

"And maybe I don't have to wait years to do it," Gary said, obviously relishing fresh dreams. "I could get my feet wet on a limited means even while I'm in school and then do it to a greater extent after I work to become established in the nursing field."

"That's true," Loralie said. "Many people here started out as 'vest pocket dealers.' They knew when the time was right to take a bigger step and turn a hobby interest into a full-time employment career."

With Gary to keep her company, and then later on to assist her as she was packing her wares, the afternoon sped by. Loralie knew she'd have to keep on a strict schedule in order not to inconvenience Denis St. John who'd graciously offered her a ride to the airport.

"Be sure to come to next year's show, Gary," Loralie said as she gave him a fond goodbye hug.

"I certainly plan to. God willing, I wouldn't miss it for the world. And, I might see you before then. I have some relatives in the Atlanta area. Quite a few uncles and an aunt. If I happen to make it down to visit them after I receive my degree—I'll look you up."

"Oh, do! I'd be sorely disappointed if you came to the vicinity and failed to make plans for us to get together. I'll look forward to the chance to someday show you around my shop."

When there was a tap at her door minutes after she'd entered her room, she found that Jon had come by to say a quick goodbye. "I really should see Denny before I leave," he said, giving his Rolex a glance.

"He's right across the hall," Loralie directed.

"Great. I'm gratified to see the changes in him, Loralie. You really seem good for him, you know that?"

She nodded. "And it feels good to feel good for him."

"Maybe you're the woman who can heal his heart. Convince him to trust again."

"If we're meant to become close friends, we will. And if not, we won't. It'll turn out as the Lord intends."

"Amen to that. Happy traveling, my friend," Jon said, and brushed a quick kiss across Loralie's smooth cheek. "I'll be in touch. I have something I want to propose to you after I get back to the office and check out a few things first."

"You have me curious," Loralie admitted.

"Sorry. But the surprise will have to wait."

"Meanie," Loralie teased.

"It's a surprise. And something that might help us to see each other again soon, if you agree to what I propose. I could find myself coming to Atlanta."

"Really, Jon?" Loralie almost squealed with excitement. "That would be so neat. I have a friend—Janeen—and I'd really love for you two to meet."

"I'll be looking forward to it. Any friend of

yours is sure to become a friend of mine."

"Don't be a stranger," Loralie said. "I hope to hear from you soon."

"Verrrrry soon," Jonathan McGuire promised.

ten

After Loralie said a quick goodbye to Jon, she hastily packed her own valise and did a double-check of the room to make sure she was not leaving any possessions behind.

She consulted her wristwatch and saw that it was minutes away from the time she'd agreed to meet Denis in the lobby to head for the airport. She was just signing her bill when Denis exited from the elevator and prepared to transact his own departure charges.

"Ready to go?"

"Any time you are," she agreed.

A cabby pulled up outside just as they were stepping onto the street and Denis signalled to him. "Lambert Field," he said curtly when they were situated inside the hired car.

The drive to the airport was quick. The taxi driver swung off the main expressway and onto the airport frontage road, then parked in front of the terminal.

"Thanks so much, Denis. And have a good trip," Loralie said, assuming he'd continue on with the cab and go to where private planes were kept in hangars.

"I don't have a specific departure time," he

said, unwinding his long legs to get out of the cab as well. "I'll come in and see you off."

"Oh! You don't have to. . . ."

"But I'd like to."

"Okay. It's a while 'til I leave."

"Great! Then we've got time for a cup of coffee in the airport restaurant."

"You got the cab. Let me get the tip—and the coffee—"

"Now, Loralie—"

"I insist," she said, "or the answer is 'no!'"

"Is that coercion?"

"Call it what you like," she invited. "It's how I conduct business."

"So Jon says."

Loralie gave Denis a searching look. Did that subtle comment mean Jon and Denis had. . .discussed her? It sounded as if they had. The idea caused mixed reactions within her.

Loralie had halfway expected Denis to offer to carry their dealer cases while she transported their suitcases, as Jon had done. When he did not suggest it, she wasn't sure if it was because he thought he might be rebuffed with a few words to the effect that she'd prefer to do it herself, or if it was because Denis was even more of a stickler about security than Jon. One of their dinner conversations the night before had centered on the need for watchful security.

The stories the dealers had had to share had been not only fascinating, they'd been frightening. Clearly, a dealer had to be on guard constantly, for frequently lone individuals, or smoothly operating teams, waited and watched for even a momentary lapse of concentration. According to all the dealers, who were united in their belief, one moment was all it took for disaster to strike.

At a show one dealer had attended, a collector had placed his inexpensive briefcase between his feet. As he'd leaned over to examine coins in the display case, he'd forgotten about the briefcase. When he prepared to move on to the next table, he looked for his case, thought maybe the dealer, an old friend, had slipped it away as a joke. He asked for his case back. The surprised dealer explained he didn't have it. Only then did they realize a problem was afoot.

Security was instantly alerted, the guards locked the doors. A search was conducted, and the briefcase—empty—and still containing the collector's identification, was found in the men's room. The culprits could have stood in the room, looking on, the coins in their pockets safe from the prying of the security guards, with it impossible for the collector to prove that the merchandise was his. Or, the professional thieves could have been out the door and lost in the crowd on the street.

Loralie's head had almost swirled from the conglomeration of crafty tricks dealers had swapped.

Denis ushered Loralie into the airport restaurant where they were seated at a quiet corner table. Loralie did as Denis did and placed her aluminum case solidly between her feet so that she could feel it with her shoes and ankles; that way no one could quickly snatch it away with her unawares.

The waitress brought them coffee, and they set about making small talk.

"Hey, Denis! How ya doin', man!" a uniformed airport employee said.

"Frank! Good to see you again."

"Are you honoring us with your presence on a flight today?" Frank asked, winking as he gave a wide grin.

"No. Sorry. I have my Cessna over in the hangar area. I'll be lifting off after I see my friend to the security equipment when it's her departure time."

"That's where I'm heading after I get a cup of coffee to go."

"See you!"

"Count on it," the smiling man said as he strode away, whistling, carefully balancing his coffee in a styrofoam cup.

"That's Frank Washington," Denis said. "I've flown so much on commercial liners that he soon came to recognize me. I attend several shows per year in St. Louis. Nice fellow. He runs the detection equipment that passengers walk through before they're allowed in the loading areas on the concourses."

"Oh, I see."

"He's good at what he does. Pleasant. But don't make a joke to Frank about having a bomb in your suitcase—or you'll find yourself in a small room with a lot of airport personnel—and there'll be nothing to laugh about. . . ."

"That's as it should be," Loralie said. "He's only doing his job."

"And the world would be a better place if everyone did their jobs with such dedicated performance."

Time seemed to pass too quickly. Loralie felt a sense of reluctance as she arose and said that she really had to prepare to go to the loading area on the green concourse.

"It's back to my normal routine for me now," she said. "What will you be doing?"

"Flying to Colorado for a few days to help out with the ANACS branch doing the authorization and certification of coins. As you know, we take photographs and do the paperwork so dealers can prove to customers that the offerings are genuine when they offer them to their clientele for sale."

"I've seen that paperwork many times, but I never realized I'd soon be meeting a man who is doing his part to be responsible for the service. It must be fascinating work."

"It has its moments. We detect a lot of fake material. And, some of it is extremely well done. In the old days some of the counterfeit material was crude. It looked and felt fake. And the weights didn't come within expected ranges at all. The average dealer could look at a coin, heft it, and get an instinctive sense that it was no good. That's no longer the case. With today's precision engineering tools, counterfeiting has become a flourishing criminal activity. The way the numismatics hobby has expanded, there aren't enough key date coins to fill the needs—so counterfeiters do it via fake material that gets into the hobby networks. Stuff good enough to pass for the real thing."

"The gold piece you labeled a fake—it certainly fooled me."

"And many others are just as good. Recently there have been some incredibly tough-to-detect counterfeits of high grade, key date coins, and gold pieces, coming out of the Orient. We don't know just where the connection results, but we know they're pipelining a lot of fake material into the United States. It's so bad that there are certain pieces, the dates they've been commonly counterfeiting to foist on collectors, where simply seeing that date show up puts our guards up. We tend to believe it's a phony until the tests convince us it's real."

"I can understand that."

"In many ways life is like that. It used to be natural for me to trust everyone else. When I was a small child, that was a way of life." He shrugged. "People were more trustworthy and ethical then.

But now there are a lot of deceitful people in circulation. And I guess that my own personal philosophy has evolved to parallel my professional view. I tend nowadays to suspect that people are fakes and phonies until they convince me that they're real and genuine. Like I think that you are. . . ."

"Well. . .thank you," Loralie said, even though she wasn't sure his comment was totally complimentary, for it sounded as if the jury was still out, and Denis St. John hadn't fully made up his mind about her basic veracity. She felt as if she was being judged. And a part of her psyche prickled with alarm when she felt that her every action was being weighed along with other behavior, and that a momentary slip of conduct could forever earn her the label of "fake and phony," deeming her a "counterfeit" human being.

"Thanks for the coffee, Loralie," Denis said as she turned away from where she'd paid the tab at the cash register.

"My pleasure. I'm glad we had these few minutes together, Denis. You're a wealth of information." She paused. "My visit to St. Louis was made more special because of your presence."

"A sentiment that's returned."

"And if you're ever in the Atlanta area and have the time, give me a call and perhaps we can get together, although I realize you're a very busy man."

"Never too busy to take a pretty lady out to dinner. Especially when she's 'one of the guys' and a coin dealer with whom I can talk shop. That's a rather appealing combination, I might admit."

Loralie stepped into line to await Frank's clearing her through the security equipment. Denis stayed at her side. With reluctance over parting, she hefted the aluminum case onto the conveyor that would run it through the X-ray equipment. It was the only time during most trips when she was traveling that it left her immediate possession. She stepped toward the metal detection equipment just as her case shot out of sight and Frank set it to the side.

The metal detection apparatus sounded a shrill alarm when Loralie stepped through, even though she was aware that she was not wearing sufficient metal to set off the alarm.

"Don't shove! Don't jostle—" Frank called out as people groaned in dismay. "This will only take a moment."

Loralie realized that just as she'd tried to slowly walk through the detection stall, she had been shoved, by the dark, almost sinister-looking man who had been standing right beside her. She thought he looked vaguely familiar. She wondered if she'd seen him at the bourse. Then, to her shock, she thought back and recalled that he was a man who'd been at the airport when she'd arrived on Wednesday evening. He'd been loitering in the arrival area and had been standing nearby when she'd told the retired AT&T executive that she was in town for a big coin show, and would be flying back to Atlanta on Sunday evening.

She realized he'd probably picked her as his victim, a small woman, a novice, and that he'd chosen to perpetrate a slick trick on her. He'd been partly in the area of the detection device's range, and she realized that very likely he had purposely had metal on him so that he'd cause the alarm to trip as she attempted to pass through. His action had set off her alarm, which caused her to be postponed for an additional check. It would result in her being detained while her coin case packed with valuable, easily liquidated items, would be on the other side, easily claimed by the thief's partner. It was a trick dealers had talked about at dinner the night before.

"Frank! *Grab him!*" Denis St. John yelled.

Recognizing Denis' voice, Frank Washington looked up. He saw a small man sidling into the crowd—with Loralie's case containing her coin inventory.

Frank yelled for additional security—and frightened, the man dropped the case with a clatter and took off, sprinting in order to lose himself in the crowd. The man who'd tripped the security system alarm realized that their carefully contrived plan had gone awry. He panicked, bolted, shoved people aside, and sprinted for the closest exit.

Loralie shuddered when she considered what could have happened had Denis not been present. The story told at the dinner table the other night had it that the accomplice, who had metal in his or her pocket, would eventually take it out and say it was "a lucky medallion" and that he or she never dared fly without it, or would present some other plausible and innocent story while the delay bought the accomplice time to escape with the purloined luggage.

Loralie was still shaking with nervousness when her trembling fingers accepted custody of her case. Her knees felt as if they were unwilling to support her as she made her way to the concourse area, still feeling almost faint from fright. It had been a close call. Much closer than she'd ever realized. Thank God that Denis had lingered near the security gate to see her safely through. And thank God that Denis was personally acquainted with Frank Washington. Thank God she hadn't just been robbed of a lifetime of numismatic acquisitions.

She realized anew how completely God *was* taking care of her. Also, He had taught her a lesson that perhaps she needed to be even less trusting where her coins were concerned. To survive in the professional world of coin collecting, where there were so many wolves in sheep's clothing, persons laden with chicanery and deceit, perhaps she needed to develop an attitude more like Denis's in some areas. Decide that anyone who came into contact with her case was a potential dishonest stranger, until actions convinced her otherwise.

By the time the jetliner was airborne, Loralie felt the tension begin to dissipate. Even so she kept the aluminum case solidly placed between her leg and her window seat. The sense of security caused her to relax in the self-contained environment so far above the midwestern land below.

The closer the aircraft drew to Atlanta, the farther away her experiences in St. Louis seemed. She found her thoughts focusing on her duties in Georgia. Her plans drifted to upcoming coin club meetings she'd be attending the following week in a nearby town. She knew a sense of enthusiasm as she faced slipping into her normal daily niche so she could attend to business as usual.

She knew she'd have a day or two of brisk work before she would feel caught up again. And she'd probably have several days of feeling unusually tired as she recovered from the late hours, long days, and general stressful hubbub she'd survived during the past week spent in the Gateway City.

It was deep evening when the 707 touched down in Atlanta. It took almost a half an hour from the time the craft first touched down on the runway until she was unlocking her car in the lot where she'd left it during her absence. Loralie locked her bag and coin inventory in the trunk, then left the lot, paid the attendant her parking fee, and headed out onto the expressway into the rather heavy Sunday evening traffic as people headed home after the weekend to gear up for another work week ahead.

She'd been going to bop in at her shop. But then she thought better of the idea. She knew she really needed to rest, and she realized that if she went by the shop it'd be too tempting to see what work awaited her, perhaps start, and "doing just one more thing" could result in her remaining at her shop half the night. She chose, instead, to just swing by the street.

She was momentarily surprised to see the lights on in her shop, although the "CLOSED" sign was solidly in place in the front window. Then when she saw Jaydee's battered old car at the curb, she relaxed, and realized that the youth was in the storefront building attending to his own business interests.

She really didn't see much of him these days. They tended not to keep the same hours. Loralie was a day person, and Jaydee because of his classes, tended to be a night person. She worked most with a face-to-face clientele at coin shows, club meetings, and at the shop. Jaydee focused on mail bid and classified advertisement contacts. Because of his needs, she was quite content to let him handle their incoming mail, since most of it was for him.

He was an early riser, up to prepare for his university classes, so two months before he had begun swinging by the post office each morning. On the way to class he'd drop off her mail promptly, and it was convenient for the both of them to allow him to handle it. Especially considering that the bulk of letter mail was for him, as were many of the trade publications he received, ranging from slick, expensive publications with large circulations on down to smeary, mimeographed efforts that went to a few hundred subscribers at best.

As Loralie thought about Jaydee, an odd youth consumed with numismatics and investments, she couldn't help comparing and contrasting him with Gary Stanley. She got along well with Jaydee. But it was strictly business with their personal boundaries severely drawn. With Gary, she realized, she'd have enjoyed such a working relationship on a more friendly and personal level.

"That's just the difference in kids," she murmured. "Jaydee's not an easy young fellow to get to know."

As she prepared for bed that night, Loralie got to thinking about her need for an assistant. Maybe Jaydee would do in a pinch. She could afford to pay his way to some closer big shows. She felt sure he'd love the environment, and that he'd enjoy dealing on his own behalf, too.

It was something to keep in mind, she decided.

She knew that she really needed someone else in her professional life. Someone to rely on.

And suddenly she realized that it was just as true in her personal life, too.

"It will happen," she comforted herself, "when the Lord intends it. And when that happens, the relationships—all of them—will be perfect. Rare and precious alliances. . . ."

eleven

Loralie had scarcely opened up her shop the next morning when the telephone shrilled.

"You're back!" Janeen gaily cried when she answered. "How was your trip?"

"It was fantastic. Sometime I'll have to tell you all about it!"

"How about now? I'm not involved in anything terribly pressing."

"If you've got the time—I'll take the time," Loralie said, and nestled down in her office chair, prepared for a pleasantly involved chat.

One of the things she enjoyed about her relationship with Janeen, in addition to a joint history that went back to high school, and a shared faith, was that Janeen was self-employed, too. Therefore, her best friend knew the ups and downs of that kind of business situation. It also gave her best girlfriend the freedom to be flexible, as to a degree, Loralie was also.

Neither of them had a boss glowering over using the telephone for personal use. Neither of them had to watch the clock. If they felt the need for time off or needed to take care of an emergency, they could put the "CLOSED" sign up in their windows. They could get together when most people had to put their own desires behind their commitments to employers. This had allowed each girl to assist the other one in a business manner, too. Janeen had helped Loralie—*gratis*—at the coin store, and when her special talents had been of use, Loralie had returned the favor.

"Meet any interesting guys?" Janeen asked.

"Interesting that you should inquire. Yes, I did. Lots of them, as a matter of fact."

"You did?"

"One for me, my dear, and also...one for you!"

"Well...do tell!" Janeen invited. "Yours first!"

Loralie sketched in her interesting relationship with Denis St. John, one that had gone from being stormy to seemingly supportive.

Then she began to sing Jonathan McGuire's praises.

"He sounds very, very nice," Janeen said when Loralie had finished listing Jonathan McGuire's attributes.

"He is. You know me, I wouldn't fix up one of my friends with...just anyone."

"I know," Janeen said. "That's why I realize that this fellow must be super-terrific. I hope we do get to meet real soon."

"Perhaps sooner than you think. Jon's talking about a business trip to Atlanta in the near future."

"Neat!"

"And I have an alternative plan should something cause his plans not to pan out. I'll be going to a show in Indianapolis next month. Since you're self-employed, and because I'd very much like you and Jon to become acquainted, and after everyone seemed to point out that I could make good use of an assistant...I thought I'd invite you to go with me. Here are the dates—so if you're game—mark 'em on your calendar."

Janeen was repeating and writing the dates in her book when Loralie's call-waiting sounded on the line.

"Hang on a moment. My call-waiting just went off. I'll click across and see who it is. Probably just a customer wanting to check to see if I'm here, or someone wanting to know my business hours."

Loralie was surprised—and delighted—when she clicked over, answered, and found Jonathan McGuire on the line.

"I have a call on the other line, Jon. Hang on a moment while I make arrangements to return the call after we're finished."

"Good enough."

Loralie clicked across. "It's him! *Jon!*" she bubbled to Janeen. "I'll let you go now—and I'll call you back as soon as we're through talking."

"Hi, Jon!" Loralie said when she clicked across again. "I knew I'd be hearing from you—but I didn't realize it would be so soon. Not that I'm complaining, mind you."

"On the flight back to Boston I found myself thinking about business—not mine, but yours. I have some ideas for you to implement if you're as serious about expanding your business as you seem to be."

"I'm open to any and all suggestions. So long as they're legal and ethical," Loralie said, laughing.

"No problems there."

Loralie listened raptly as Jon talked about the ins and outs of the business, explaining that walk-in business for a dealer had built-in limits caused by considerations such as locale, population, store hours, et cetera.

"To really expand you need to hit the national market. But you can't spend all your time or overhead attending shows, of course. So you can do it by using computerization and also setting up mail-bid auctions that you distribute to interested persons on a national level."

"That sounds really good, Jon. But the idea of keeping all those records, and attending to all that paperwork almost gives me the vapors."

"That's the surprise I was talking about. Our firm just bought a new state-of-the-art mainframe setup with a number of individual terminals. We had a custom-made program created for our specific needs. That means that we have an older, but perfectly good, computer system and program for which we no longer have a need."

"Oh. . . ." Loralie said, seeing the direction in which Jon was leading.

"I'd like for you to have it," Jon said. "I'd sooner see it go to someone who'd use, enjoy, and benefit from it, than to have it gather dust and take up space in a storage room. It's yours, Loralie, along with my best wishes for your continued success."

"I can't just take it for nothing."

"But I want you to have it."

"Only if you'll let me purchase it, Jon. I know what it'd cost me to set myself up with new equipment and a program."

"Okay. If you insist."

"Name a price, Jon."

"How about a meal or two while I'm in Atlanta, and a sightseeing tour around the Civil War monuments and battlefields."

"That's all?"

"That's more than enough."

"That's easily enough handled. You won't complain if I make it a threesome, will you?"

"With your friend Janeen?"

"Uh-huh."

"I was rather hoping you might suggest it. Your high recommendation speaks well of her. I know you don't give such praise lightly. I've found myself really looking forward to meeting her."

"She's looking forward to making your acquaintance, too. In fact, Janeen had just called to see how the show had gone. I was in the midst of telling her about you when you called."

"Well, tell her that God willing I'll be meeting her very soon. I can bring the computer to Atlanta, and even though we'll be busy doing fun things, we can allot enough time for me to give you some hands-on instruction so that before I hop a flight back to Boston, I can reassure myself that you're safely up and running."

"You're a treasure."

"You're going to love the set-up, Loralie. It's like being able to add several dedicated, trustworthy, low-overhead employees—without the overhead and hassles."

"I could use that," Loralie said. "I realize that I can no longer rely on just myself and the services of Janeen, and what little Jaydee does around my shop that does assist me. I thank the Lord that you've come into my life in a professional capacity as well as a personal one."

"How does the weekend after next sound to you?" Jon asked. "I could fly down then if your calendar is clear and it's agreeable with you."

"Let me check," Loralie said, fearing that she'd be booked with a monthly show or other commitment. But when she glanced ahead at the pages of her planner she saw it was free of all obligations.

"You're on! It's perfect. And if God smiles on us—the weather will be, too. Let me know what time your flight is coming in and I—and maybe Janeen—can be at the airport to meet you."

"Until then, Loralie."

"I'll be counting the days. As, I'm sure Janeen will be, too." Loralie was just preparing to dial Janeen's number when Jaydee came into the shop with a batch of outgoing packages boxed up awaiting the UPS deliveryman's arrival.

"You've been a busy, busy boy," Loralie said.

"I sure have. This mail order aspect is really a gold mine," he said. "I'm rolling in money. I'm thinking about replacing my old clunker with something upscale and impressive."

"So it seems mail order dealing is lucrative. I may be investigating that myself," Loralie said.

"Oh really?" Jaydee murmured.

She thought she caught the flash of a frown slip across his features, but when she looked again it was gone, and she believed she'd been mistaken.

"Don't worry, there's plenty of business for the both of us."

"Right," he said. "Listen, I have the check made out for the UPS man, so simply fill in the amount, make a note of it, and I'll write it in my check register when I pick up the invoice."

"Will do!" Loralie agreed.

"I went by the post office," Jaydee said. He extracted a few business size envelopes and several weekly publications that had arrived. "Here's your mail."

"Looks like you kept the PO clerks busy all by yourself," Loralie said when she saw the sheaf of first class mail, and a healthy stack of trade publications that Jaydee was obviously going to take back to his apartment with him.

"Busy enough," he admitted. "See you around!"

"Don't take any wooden nickels," Loralie warned.

"Don't bother to make any of them, either," Jaydee teased back. "There's really no money in them. . . ."

twelve

The next two weeks sped by. Loralie saw very little of Jaydee except when he came to the shop in order to drop off what usually amounted to a box of outgoing padded mailer packets he used to send out coins to fill customers' orders.

Loralie noticed his eyes sometimes seemed red-rimmed, and that he yawned a lot and sometimes complained of eyestrain until Loralie suggested he get his glasses prescription checked again, and pay attention to lighting when he studied his textbooks.

"Beware of burning the candles at both ends," she warned. "You can't keep this up forever, you know."

"I don't intend to," he said. "But I graduate in two months, and I'll probably be leaving the area, so I want to really work my business before I make arrangements to move away from Atlanta."

"Good idea," Loralie said. "It'll be like money in the bank if you have a lengthy mailing list of satisfied customers when you get ready to do another mail bid or ad campaign. The nice thing about your set-up is you don't have to establish a whole new clientele— just be sure to take your mailing list along, and you're right back in business."

Jaydee gave an undecipherable grunt, and rushed out the door, presumably to class.

She was kept busy herself that day, and she scarcely paid any attention when the UPS man came to collect outgoing parcels. She paused only long enough to present Jaydee's check in payment and to file the receipt so the young man could have it for his records.

It seemed that every waking moment of her time was involved in thought—thoughts about why she hadn't heard from Denis. Thoughts about the things Jon had said she should do to prepare to switch over to an electronic system to aid her. And making back-of-the-mind plans in order that in two days when Jon arrived in the Queen City of the South, his stay would be memorable.

Finally the big day came.

Janeen wasn't free to go to the airport with Loralie to collect Jon from the terminal, but Loralie had made reservations for dinner that included her best girlfriend.

"Jon! How great to see you!" Loralie cried. She gave him a warm hug as he exited from the concourse area. "My car is waiting. We'll be en route as soon as we get your luggage."

They made small talk as they proceeded toward the terminal. The conveyor disgorged Jon's suitcase that Loralie recognized, then a moment later a solidly wrapped and very chunky box spewed from the ramp and onto the carousel.

"Get my valise, if you don't mind, and I'll carry the computer," Jon said.

"You've got a deal."

Minutes later they paused by the rear of Loralie's

compact car. She raised the trunk lid, and they placed Jon's suitcase and the computer in the storage well.

"If you'll run me by my hotel, I'll get checked in," Jon said. "Then perhaps we can drop off the computer at your shop."

Loralie consulted her wristwatch. "That should work out very well. By the time we accomplish all that, Janeen should be ready to join us. We shouldn't keep late hours tonight, though, because we're planning for you to have a grand tour of Atlanta and the immediate environs tomorrow."

"I'm really looking forward to it," Jon said. "That's the way to see any city—view it with a native."

"I agree."

"Perhaps I can reciprocate when you get a chance to visit Boston."

Loralie parked in front of the hotel, then waited in the lobby as Jon filled out paperwork, took possession of his room key, went up to drop off his suitcase, then returned to the lobby.

"It's about a ten-minute drive to my shop," Loralie said. "And please don't entertain any grandiose expectations. I know that it can't compare to McGuire Coin Galleries."

"I'm not impressed by appearances if there's nothing to offer beneath the glittering facade," Jon reminded. "And as for modest beginnings—my grandfather was a true 'vest pocket' dealer. It wasn't until my father went into business with him that they actually opened a bona fide shop. We have pictures of it hanging in our building to remind us of the humble beginnings. It was a true hole-in-the-wall enterprise."

"I feel better," Loralie admitted, giving a laugh.

"We have that picture hanging in our present-day complex we had specially constructed a few years ago to remind us of the humble beginnings we came from—and to warn us where we could return to if we don't maintain our business' sterling reputation."

"How true," Loralie said. "McGuire Coin Gallery has an exemplary reputation. And in this business a good name can be worth a lot."

"So many people have been burned by bad and deceitful dealings that most collectors approach new dealers with a patina of distrust. And when they discover that a dealer is trustworthy and honest, then they seem to let down their guards and become loyal, sometimes willing to pay a bit more to have that reputation of honesty than seek out bargains and get burned in the process."

"Here we are!" Loralie said. She parked on the nearly deserted street and fished her keys from a side pocket of her leather purse.

"Appealing," Jon said. "And the layout is super. You've made really efficient use of what space you have available."

"Janeen was a great help to me there," Loralie admitted. "She's in that business. So she quite naturally thinks in those kinds of terms."

For the next half an hour Loralie showed Jon around her shop, pulling trays of coins from the safe, sharing with him some especially fine specimens of which she was very proud.

"Excuse me a moment while I call Janeen's apartment to see if she's returned. If she has then we'll swing by, pick her up, and make our way to the restaurant."

"Terrific," Jon said. "I'm famished."

"She's back—and raring to go," Loralie said when she returned a moment later from her office. "Her apartment is only about five minutes from here."

Janeen was standing in the vestibule of her apartment building. When she saw Loralie drive up to the curb, she exited the building.

"Hi, all!" she said in a cheery tone as she hastily entered Loralie's car, buckling in.

"Janeen, this is Jonathan McGuire of McGuire Coin Gallery in Boston. Jon, this is Janeen Ross. She's self-employed as an interior decorator and design consultant."

"Hi, Janeen, I'm pleased to meet you," Jon said and swiveled around to extend his hand.

"My pleasure," Janeen said.

"I've heard so many nice things about you," Jon said. "Loralie has really sung your praises."

"Her behavior has been duplicated with me on your behalf. It's neat that we're finally getting to meet. I feel, in many ways, as if I already know you."

Talk came easily. The restaurant ambience was conducive to intimate, friendly conversation. The food was sumptuous, with Loralie wondering if the chefs had really outdone their own past efforts, or if the delectable items only seemed more tasty because their dining pleasure was intensified by the enjoyable company they were keeping.

Loralie quietly slipped away to take care of the bill. Then they lingered over a second cup of coffee, then a third.

"We really should call it a night. We've got a full day planned for tomorrow."

"Dinner's on me tomorrow night," Jon stipulated. "We'll have to allow time to set up the computer and install the program and give you time to acquaint yourself."

"Tomorrow night?"

"We'll plan on it."

"Don't make any plans, Janeen," Loralie said, "for I'd like you to be around when Jon explains it to me. I might never know when I'd need your help."

"Okeydoke," she agreed. "Count me in."

It was after ten o'clock in the evening when Loralie and Janeen dropped Jon off in front of his downtown hotel.

"You didn't exaggerate," Janeen sighed as Loralie zipped away from the curb and into the Friday night traffic. "The man is a dream come true!"

Loralie gave a pleased chuckle. "Didn't I tell you as much? And I know Jon well enough to know that he's as impressed with you as you are with him."

"You know, Loralie," Janeen said, and her tone was solemn. "I have a really good feeling about this relationship."

"Me, too," Loralie admitted. "Deep down I feel that it's one that might be a love meant to be."

"If you ever tire of coin-dealing, you could always

hang out a shingle and offer your services as a matchmaker. You seem to have talents that make you a natural."

"For others, perhaps, but not for myself. . . ."

"Denis St. John still hasn't called you?" Janeen asked.

Loralie gave a quick shake of her head. "Not yet."

"Give him time. I'm sure he will."

"I'm not. Maybe to him it was like a cruise ship relationship. Nice while it lasted. But over as soon as we parted."

"Don't be negative, Lor. Maybe he simply lost your business card."

"That might be. But he knows how to find me if he wants to."

"You've said that he's not the marrying kind. If he feels about you as you seem to be feeling about your attraction to him, it may be scaring him."

"You could be right. Or it might be all wrong."

"Why don't you ask Jon about him?"

"Maybe I will. If I get the chance."

"We're all going to be together as we do the city and the sights tomorrow. As much as you've done to assist my cause with your matchmaking efforts, the least I can do is create a smooth opening for you to quite naturally inquire about one Denis St. John. Right?"

"If you say so."

"Janeen has spoken!" she decided, her tone inarguable.

thirteen

The next morning Loralie arose at dawn so she could hastily attend to necessary duties in order to free herself for a day spent sight-seeing with Jon and Janeen.

On the way to Jon's hotel, Loralie picked up Janeen, then proceeded downtown. To spare them the inconvenience of parking, Jon was outside, chatting with the uniformed doorman, watching for their arrival.

Loralie double-parked in the street long enough for him to climb in. "I'll drive, and Janeen can serve as the tour director," she said.

Jon laughed. "That's an equitable division of labor. I'll serve as the enthusiastic Yankee tourist."

"Now that we all know our assigned roles—we're off!" Loralie said and shifted into gear as she pulled into the Saturday morning traffic.

Janeen began to explain the state's history, as she'd learned it in grade school. "Our state, of course, is famous for cotton, magnolia trees, and peaches—"

"And very pretty girls," Jon inserted, winking, as he flashed each girl a grin.

"Our fair city, Atlanta, also serves as the state capitol. Its history can be seen in the Cyclorama, a large, modernistic edifice, housing a vast, circular,

146

and extremely life-like painting of the battle action which took place in the general vicinities of Atlanta proper.

"One of the sites to be seen in the Cyclorama is 'Five Points', which was mentioned in the novel *Gone with the Wind*. The location is now in the heart of the financial district.

"Five Points became the turn-around location for Georgia's first railroad. The little town which sprang up there was referred to as 'Terminus.' Later on, Terminus' name was changed and it was then referred to as 'Marthasville,' and then in 1847, it was called 'Atlanta'. It was a growing city by then, but it did not become our state capital until 1868, when it was tentatively selected, then affirmed on a permanent basis in 1877."

"How interesting," Jon said. "I had no idea."

"Today Atlanta is considered the 'headquarter city' of the entire southeastern region. Many national brand name business and industrial firms maintain thousands of branch, district, and division offices for their firms right here in our city. And in addition to that, government is also an important aspect in the city, for Atlanta is also the location of Fulton County government and state interests, not to mention the many branches of federal agencies that conduct business from major offices in Atlanta."

"It's really lovely."

"It is," Loralie agreed with Jon. "This is my favorite time of year in Georgia."

"Our climate is basically easy to accept all year

long," Janeen said.

"In another minute or two," Loralie said, "I'll be driving by the state's capitol off to your right."

"Take special note of it, Jon, for the capitol's dome is covered with Georgia gold. We don't have time to go inside today—not if we're going to take in the itinerary that Lor and I have planned for our day. But one of the capitol's most interesting sections is the State Museum of Natural History, located on the fourth floor, if you return to Atlanta and have time to pay it a visit."

"Everyone has heard of Georgia Tech," Loralie said. "My associate, Jaydee, attends classes here. It's a leading engineering school, of course, and is also noted for football greatness, as well as scholastic fame."

For several hours the girls showed Jon around the city. They stopped for lunch in an ethnic restaurant, then enjoyed an afternoon's sight-seeing while venturing toward their destination, Stone Mountain, a short distance east of Atlanta.

"Stone Mountain creates North America's largest exposed granite formation, Jon, and is one of the world's natural wonders. Just below its summit, you'll see the imposing memorial to the Confederacy that was carved in the rock by Gutzon Borglum, the famous sculptor also responsible for the Black Hills Memorial.

"At the site, an exact replica of the Civil War engine, 'The General', transports tourists around the mountain. A skylift carries them to the top where there is a small museum and concession shops."

"I'll park and we can get out, walk around, and if you desire, do the tourist routine along with the others visiting Stone Mountain today," Loralie said.

The trio was tired, their hair wind-tossed, their skin rosy from the effects of the late spring sun when they returned to Loralie's car.

"I'm glad the dinner hour is approaching," Jon said. "I'm really starving."

"Me, too," Loralie agreed.

"Make it unanimous."

"What do y'all say that we buzz back to the city, get ready, and go out to dine right away so that we can arrive before the busy dinner hour?"

"Good idea. That will allow us to return to your shop so we can set up the computer system."

"You're right. We really shouldn't postpone it any longer," Loralie agreed.

"Postpone?" Jon inquired, cocking an eyebrow. "Do I hear some evidence of human distrust of an electronic contraption?"

"Things mechanical are not my forte."

"The program is user-friendly, Loralie. You'll be surprised how quickly you come to view that computer system as your best buddy and most agreeable employee!"

After a lovely dinner and a few minutes relaxing over coffee, the trio headed for the Morgan Coin shop.

Loralie unlocked the doors, deactivated the alarm system, flipped on the lights, and led the way into the office where Jon had stowed the box containing the computer.

Loralie and Jan made small talk as they watched Jon hook up computer cables, plug the device into a socket, then turn it on. He hummed under his breath as he programmed it, asked Loralie to type in a password, then he continued on with the installation. In a calm, clear voice he began explaining the basics of computer programming to the women.

He kept the concepts simple, and Loralie was amazed how quickly she grasped the idea, even as she fretted that she wouldn't remember the details and necessary commands come morning.

"I'll be leaving a program manual," Jon said. "If you have a problem—help is as close as the phone. Tell me what the problem is and chances are I can 'talk you through it.' In addition, I've prepared a 'cheat sheet' of the most necessary and frequently used commands. Who wants to try first?"

"It's her rig," Janeen said. "She should."

Loralie seated herself, and with Jon's coaching, worked her way through some computer program functions with only a few misbobbles. After about ten minutes, her head was already swirling at the possibilities for saving time and effort.

"Your turn, Janeen!" Loralie said, hopping from the seat.

Janeen, who had absorbed many commands while watching Loralie perform, seemed a natural.

It was almost eleven o'clock when the group turned as they heard a key in the front door. Jaydee came in, looking surprised to find so many people in the shop.

Janeen he'd met, Jon he had not, and Loralie felt he viewed the older man with a look of hesitant suspicion, which seemed to increase when she introduced Jon, complete with a rundown of his professional numismatic memberships and affiliations.

"Pleased to meet you, sir," Jaydee said, stiffly extending his hand. As he did so, he dropped a roll of Lincoln cents. Jon was quick to retrieve them.

"Mind if I take a look at them?"

". . .No. . . ."

Jon, seeming to notice the youth's discomfort, attempted to draw him out.

"What are they?"

"Those? Uh..just some 1914 Lincolns," Jaydee said.

"Just buy them?"

"Well, yeah. They came in the mail today."

Seeming almost reluctant, he watched the well-known coin dealer spill a few of them from the tube into the palm of his hand. Jon scrutinized them, then restacked them in the plastic coin tube, twisted the lid back on, and handed them back.

"Nice coins," he said. "Too bad they're not 1914 D's, huh?"

"No lie," Jaydee said, and then a strained silence fell among them as Jaydee puttered in his area and seemed antsy for them to go.

"Time to call it a night," Loralie said, yawning. "If we don't bring the day to a close soon we'll be able to go straight from the shop to church services in the morning."

"Right you are," Janeen said.

"I'll leave a wake-up call at the desk. Brunch after services are on me," Jon said. "And maybe we can have a bit of time afterwards to hang out before I have to head for the airport. I can take a cab from the hotel."

"Nonsense!" Loralie said. "I can take you to the terminal. . .unless Janeen would like to do the honors."

Loralie had seen the looks and special rapport that had passed between her friends. She sensed that they longed to spend at least a little time together—alone.

"I-I guess I could take Jon to the airport," Janeen shyly agreed.

"I do have a few things to attend to around my apartment," Loralie smoothly explained.

"Thanks!" Jon and Janeen said in unison, causing Loralie to laugh.

Then she grew serious as she realized that time was fast running out for her to "casually" inquire of Jon about Denis.

"So. . .have you heard from Denis St. John lately?"

"As a matter of fact, yes. I probably should've told you, because no doubt you've been waiting to hear from him."

"Well, actually, yes, I have been."

"He's been terribly busy at the ANACS headquarters. And he's had speaking engagements to fulfill. The man has more duties to attend to than he has hours in which to perform them. But he's giving up some offices in national coin associations, and he's hoping to have more time to attend to his own needs then. For a man like Denis St. John, his personal world gets short shrift compared to his professional existence. I suspect you'll hear from him shortly. Maybe after the weekend. He knew we were going to spend it together, so I figure maybe he'll choose to call after I've returned to Boston to allow us uninterrupted time together this weekend."

"I hope he does call."

"I would believe that you'll hear from him soon. If he doesn't call you—you can phone him," Jon reminded. "He's a very busy man. Although I think he's giving serious thought to settling down. None of us are mere kids any more."

"I won't call him," Loralie said. "If I'm meant to hear from him, I will—and if I'm not, I won't."

But even as she expressed the sentiment, a rebellious part of her heart fervently hoped Denis St. John would call—and soon!

fourteen

Sunday morning Loralie rushed to collect both Janeen and Jon for church. The services were inspiring, and Loralie enjoyed introducing her friend from Boston to her local church family.

Following the morning worship services, the trio went for a late brunch, then Loralie took Jon and Janeen to the latter's apartment. Loralie and Jon said a quick farewell, then she departed, leaving her friend to see Jon to the airport later.

Loralie was tired, but felt good about the weekend as she returned to her apartment to catch up on a few things that needed her attention. She had a light supper, showered, and was writing a letter, when the telephone rang. She suspected it might be Janeen, phoning her to report on her time spent alone with Jon.

Loralie was not expecting to have Denis St. John's voice greet her ears. "Well, what a pleasant surprise," she said.

"Sorry it took me so long to contact you," Denis said. "I've really been busy."

"That's what Jon said."

"How did your weekend go?"

"Like a dream come true. He really enjoyed touring the city, and Jon and my best friend seemed to hit it

154

off."

"That's nice. He told you that I talked to him last week?"

"As a matter of fact, he did."

"Been keeping busy?"

"Almost impossibly so," Loralie answered.

"Orders really rolling in from the mail order business?"

"Not yet," Loralie laughed. "I've only just begun, you know. Jon taught Janeen and me how to run the program last night."

". . .Oh, I'd have thought you'd have had time to know how the 'draw' went by now."

Loralie wasn't sure what Denis was talking about; she believed he was somehow confused, but rather than risk arguing the point, she changed the subject.

She was startled when her call-waiting went off, and she looked at her watch to realize that almost two hours had elapsed since she'd picked up the telephone to find Denis on the line.

"I'd better let you go. My call-waiting beep just sounded. And if we don't end this call soon, you're going to end up owning the telephone company."

"I think I already should. Last month's bill looked like figures for the national debt."

"I know the feeling. Thanks for calling, Denis. I really enjoyed it."

"We'll talk again. Soon!"

"Bye!"

Quickly Loralie clicked over. Janeen was on the line. "I was just about to give up and try later, figuring you didn't want to interrupt a call when your answering machine didn't come on with the fourth ring."

"I've been talking to Denis."

"He called!"

"Yes, two hours ago. . . ."

"Whew! You had a lot to talk about. Or were you arguing?" Janeen teased.

"Actually, we got along very amicably, although I suppose we could've fought. He seemed to have the idea in his head that I've already been doing mail order business. He must've got his wires crossed. He really seemed to have an expression in his voice as if I was misleading him with my denials. But if so— that's his problem."

"Do you think you'll be seeing him soon?"

"At the Indianapolis show for sure. Maybe before then. And if not, I do have a feeling that he'll call again."

"You could call him. . . ."

Loralie shook her head. "Not until he's phoned me several times first. I have to. . .maintain the boundaries. . .of this relationship. I guess I don't quite trust Denis like I would wish to. And I certainly won't have him believing that I'm. . .chasing him!"

"I can understand that."

"So how did it go with Jon?"

"Loralie, the man's a treasure. Thank you, thank you, thank you for laying the groundwork to bring us together. I just hated to see him get on the airplane."

"So, I'll field the same question to you: Do you think you'll be seeing him soon?"

"Well, for sure in Indianapolis—"

"You've decided to accompany me?" Loralie cried.

"Uh-huh. I was leaning in that direction on the strength of your suggestion. But Jon's input was the clincher."

"We're going to have so much fun. I can hardly wait."

"And, there's a solid chance that I may see Jon in as few as three weeks—"

"Do tell!"

"Two weeks ago I got a flyer about a trade show in Boston for interior decorators. It's a huge production with reps from furniture companies, carpet mills, drapery factories, producers of accessories. The whole nine yards. I was kind of wanting to go, but not feeling I could really justify it."

"Ah, and now Jon helps justify it."

"Mmmmmhmmmm. And the trade show also helps justify going to see Jon when we've just met."

"Nothing like combining business with pleasure."

"It's kind of a neat way to live, isn't it?"

"Very much so," Loralie agreed. "I have a kazillion and one things to do to prepare for the Indianapolis show."

"And I have to buy some new clothes to go to Boston."

"We're going to be some very busy women in the near future," Loralie predicted.

"But not too busy to talk to our male friends if they call."

And call they did.

Janelle and Loralie had limited time to talk to each other on the telephone, because after the first week they discovered that when their schedules allowed, Jon and Denis called the girls almost nightly, even if all they could manage was a few minutes to say hello. Other nights the calls were extended, and both Loralie and Janeen felt pleased at how the long-distance relationships were developing.

"Ready for your big weekend in Boston?"

"At last!" Janeen admitted. "I just wish that you were going along."

"I have things to do around here," Loralie said. "And there's always the show in Indy to prepare for."

"I'm going to feel a bit sad that I'm off in Boston in Jon's company, while you're here in Atlanta and Denis is going to be who-knows-where."

"I'm not sure where he's going to be this weekend. He really hasn't said. Last time he phoned he was calling from Colorado. He was at the American Numismatic Association headquarters. I know that the ANACS duties are keeping him busy. It seems they've had a spate of fakes flooding the market."

"At least you'll get to see him when we're in Indy," Janeen commiserated.

Friday night, Loralie found her thoughts drifting north to Bean Town, as she wondered how the reunion between Janeen and Jon was going. Saturday, when she was at the shop waiting on customers, her thoughts kept returning to her friends who she believed were quickly falling in love with one another.

Her musings were forced away from the pair when

she did a brisk business on Saturday evening. Right near closing time the bell above the door tinkled.

Loralie was in her office to the rear. "Be with you in a moment," she sang out.

She walked through the door to the showroom and her mouth dropped open with surprise. There stood Denis St. John!

"Wh-what are you doing here?!" she cried.

"I had some problems with my Cessna. The mechanics told me it'd be a couple of hours. When I get back they should have it repaired, refueled, and ready to go. So I thought I'd surprise you."

"You certainly did."

"Any chance you're free to go out for dinner tonight?"

"Although a woman isn't supposed to let a fellow know she's got nothing better to do on a Saturday night than give herself a shampoo and manicure, I'm forthright enough to admit I have no plans. I'd love to go out for dinner."

"Great. How soon until closing time?"

Loralie crossed the showroom in quick steps and flipped the sign. "Right now!"

"I like your sense of priorities, Loralie. Where shall we go?" Loralie named several excellent eating establishments. "Take your pick."

Denis made his selection. "We'll take my rental car. We can leave yours at the shop, and I'll bring you here later."

"Okeydoke!"

Loralie felt almost as if she was dreaming when

Denis helped her into the luxury rental car and pulled away from the curb. The way he negotiated the streets, she realized he knew the city well, and she observed as much.

"I had relatives here, all passed on now. Mother, Father, and I used to come to big shows here. So I have a general sense of direction from the old days that's stood me in good stead each time I've visited Atlanta on business."

Talk between them was easy. Denis was charming, attentive, and Loralie felt almost as if their initial unpleasant encounters had been a bad dream. It seemed almost impossible that the man who was so courtly and gallant now could have ever been so ill-behaved.

"I'd better be heading back to the airport. This has been nice. . . ."

Then, as if she were moving in slow motion, almost in a dream state, Loralie felt herself pulled toward Denis, as he seemed drawn to her, and suddenly their lips met with all the snug perfection of which she'd dreamed.

The effect on her was immediate and intense.

Denis was no less affected. "Sweet," he murmured in a husky tone. "So sweet. Don't ever change. . . ."

Loralie's heart was racing when Denis said that it was time to go.

"I'll be leaving for home soon," she said.

"You're not departing right away?"

"I was going to get into the shop to make sure everything's in order. I left pretty quickly this afternoon."

"For security's sake, I'll go in with you. A few minutes won't make any difference."

"I'd like that."

Loralie did a few chores around the shop and was ready to turn on the alarm system and get out her keys to lock up, when a car pulled up out front. She glanced out, but didn't recognize the vehicle.

It was a bright, cherry red, low slung sports model. Her brow wrinkled in concern, until she saw Jaydee's lanky form and recognized his mad-scientist mop of unruly hair. She opened the door to him before he could reach for his key.

"Hello, Jaydee," Loralie said. "I was just getting ready to leave. I'd like you to meet a caller to the coin shop. Denis St. John—he works with the ANACS branch of the ANA. He's written a book on counterfeit detection. He's one of the foremost experts in the coin business."

For a moment Jaydee's complexion seemed to grow pale. Then he collected himself, extended his hand, and made a few mumblings.

Denis, viewing the young man as a friend of Loralie's, went out of his way to get polite conversation going. Even when Jaydee seemed reluctant, Denis pressed him about his class load, the courses of study he was taking, and his plans for his life after he graduated with his degree in engineering.

"I don't know what I'll do. Probably leave Atlanta. Engineers are in demand overseas, and in South America and other exotic places."

"The pay can be tempting, but being an expatriate is a difficult existence." As Loralie did a few things around the shop, Denis made conversation with Jaydee, asking a lot of what seemed almost probing questions. Jaydee answered, but seemed resentful. He began making excuses that he had a few things to do before he kept an appointment with a friend, so he was sorry he didn't have more time to talk.

"I'll be leaving now, Jaydee," Loralie said.

"Interesting meeting you, Jaydee," Denis said. "I have a hunch we'll be seeing more of one another."

Suddenly there seemed an edge to Denis' voice, a hard, flat tone that she hadn't encountered since they'd clashed during their worst moments in St. Louis. She couldn't imagine what had caused Denis to suddenly become brooding, the expression on his face almost sinister.

Surely he wasn't jealous of Jaydee? But something had certainly struck an unpleasant chord in him.

She realized there was little she could do about Denis' quicksilver attitudes, except give him the benefit of the doubt and continue to live by her own principles. But as she drifted off to sleep that night she felt almost haunted by the collage of faces that peopled her thoughts.

Jaydee's strained face.

Denis' suspicious scowl.

Jaydee's nervous glances.

Denis' piercing stare.

Jaydee's sudden lack of confidence.

Denis' almost over-bearing questioning of the youth

that he had tried to pass off as polite chitchat.

Something was going on. . . .

Loralie didn't know what it was. But she sensed that time would tell, and she hoped whatever the undercurrent passing between Jaydee and Denis, it would not be the catalyst to implode her growing relationship with Denis St. John.

fifteen

Loralie went to the airport to meet Janeen's incoming flight on Sunday night.

"How was your trip?"

"Super!"

"Did they feed you on the airplane?"

"No. And I'm starving."

"How does McDonald's sound?"

"Like manna from heaven."

"Okeydoke. My treat," Loralie said.

Several minutes later, Loralie wheeled in when she saw the familiar golden arches. The girls placed their orders, collected their trays, then took a quiet corner booth.

"So," Loralie said, taking a bite of her sandwich. "How was the trade show? And how was Jon?"

For the next five minutes Janeen gave a euphoric monologue about Jon, the trade show, Boston, and the members of the McGuire family she had met.

"I'm so happy for you," Loralie told her. "It's been a weekend for you to remember."

"You know how I've spent the last forty-eight hours. Anything interesting take place in your life since I departed our fair city for points north?"

"As a matter of fact. . .yes," Loralie admitted, scarcely able to contain a grin.

"Well. . .do tell!"

"Denis stopped in for a few hours on Saturday night, and we went out for dinner."

"You're kidding! What a neat surprise that must've been. But only for a few hours? Did you have any idea that he was arriving in Atlanta?"

"He'd planned only to refuel his Cessna, but he said he was having some problem with his airplane, so he was detained while the mechanics did some repair work."

"That was nice. Not nice that his aircraft was malfunctioning, but pleasant that it got you two together again, if that's what it took to do the trick."

"I was glad to see him. It'll make it easier to pick up where we left off at the St. Louis coin show."

"So how was he?"

"He looked wonderful, although a bit strained. He's been keeping a rigorous schedule. I worry that he's not taking enough time for himself."

"What kind of news did he have?"

"Not a lot. The best news he had, at least as I saw it, was when he said that he'd been taking time from his busy schedule to attend church services no matter where he's at."

"No kidding? Loralie, that's great!"

"It makes me very happy. And I know that Jon will be relieved to learn of it, too. He's known Denis for many years and when we were in St. Louis, Jon told me he's been praying for Denis for quite some time."

"I hope that his prayers will be answered in full," Janeen said.

"I hope so, too. . . . Denis is a powerful man. And sometimes. . .hard. I know he has to be in some instances. He's a proud man. Of course, we all have our areas of pride. I guess what I'm trying to say is that I realize for him to feel convicted, and to become so humbled that he realizes he's powerless except for the strength found in the Lord, it's going to take a lot." She paused. "I'm hopeful, but not entirely optimistic, for a sudden change of heart. Even though I do see it as a positive change that he's attending worship services."

"That would seem to indicate that his heart is hungering for the Lord. That he's seeking goodness and righteousness in his life."

"We can be there as his friends, encouraging him with our Christian behavior. Perhaps it will make him aware that he wants the kind of personal relationship with his Savior that we all cherish."

"Won't it be fun when the four of us can be together in Indianapolis?"

"It'll be like a dream come true."

"To think that I'll be seeing Jon—and you'll be seeing Denis again—and in less than two weeks."

"I've already booked our suite and have the confirmation number."

"After being your friend for so long, and now meeting Jon, I'm finding that I'm really getting interested in the coin-collecting hobby."

"That's good," Loralie teased. "The day may come when Jon McGuire will be very grateful to me. You'll be table-sitting for me in Indy—and if the day comes when you two may take the big step that I see likely in your future—he can thank me for handing you over properly trained!"

"Oh...you!" Janeen teased, blushing as she grinned. "Actually," she said, fluffing her long dark hair, "I was thinking along those lines myself."

"Jon probably is, too."

"If things work out for you and Denis—what would *you* do?" Janeen countered.

"I don't know. But where there's love and a shared faith," Loralie said, "two hearts in perfect harmony always find a way. . . ."

Business was good the following week, both buying and selling. Loralie was elated, for it meant that she'd have plenty of cash with which to purchase items for resale. And what she bought nicely increased her inventory that she could take to the Indianapolis bourse.

She was surprised when she received a card from Gary Stanley. When she saw the return address she was flooded with sudden warm feelings. The card lifted her spirits, but not nearly so much as the news it contained.

Gary was going to make the three-hour drive to Indianapolis so that he could visit with his new friends in the numismatic industry.

"You'll like him," Loralie assured Janeen when she told her. "What's he like?"

"He's in nursing school at Southern Illinois University, Edwardsville. It's located not far from East St. Louis. Gary graduates in June. I'll have to remember to get him a little memento to mark the occasion."

"He must be about Jaydee's age, hmmmm?"

"I believe so. Jaydee graduates soon, too. I suppose I should also get him something. It's hard to think of what to give to him."

"Lately, it seems he buys whatever he wants," Janeen said thoughtfully. "Those kinds of people are the most difficult to select gifts for."

"Gary should be easy. He's endearingly grateful for even the smallest kindnesses."

"He must not be anything like Jaydee."

"Oh, they're as different as day and night. Both of them likeable enough, but—"

"I don't think Jaydee's all that likeable, Loralie. I know that you've become at least a little fond of him. But, quite frankly, he leaves me cold."

"He's different. But frequently exceptionally intelligent people are. He's in MENSA, you know, that society for geniuses."

"He may be intelligent—but he's clearly not smart enough to have many social graces."

"Perhaps he's got his mind on loftier thoughts," Loralie defended her associate.

Janeen gave what was almost a rude snort.

Loralie looked at her. "You really don't like Jaydee, do you?"

"I don't know that it's that I don't like him," she said, and there was a reflective tone to her voice. "I guess it would be more honest and accurate to say that there's simply something about him that I don't trust. With him, I feel it's not a case of 'what you see is what you get.' I always feel as if there's something about him that he keeps carefully hidden."

"That mop of hair hides a lot. Including most of his face at times," Loralie made an offhand remark.

"What are you going to do when he leaves Atlanta?

I heard him say that once he graduated he'd be moving on."

"Well, new engineers usually have to go where the jobs are," Loralie said. "I'm not sure what I will do. Nothing, for a while, that is. The computer Jon so graciously gave me is equal to having another person in the shop. But if I am going to expand the business the way I'd like, I really do need a warm body—and a knowledgeable one—to run the shop when I'm away. I'm already committing myself to shows for the autumn and winter months. And it's a scientific impossibility for the same person to be in two different places at the same time."

"Something will work out," Janeen assured. "I'll add that intention to my prayer list, and request that my prayer partners do, too."

"Thanks," Loralie said. "And if you haven't already, I'd appreciate it, and I know Jon would, if you'd pray for Denis St. John to surrender his life to the Lord."

"It's already been done. But I'll turn my prayer partners loose on that one, too, if you'd like."

"I'd be eternally grateful. . . ."

"Enough said. Consider it done."

"Even if Denis and I aren't meant to be, I am fond of him, and I care about him enough to want him to have the best. And all the grace and guidance that the Lord has to give . . . ."

sixteen

"We're going to have to hurry, Lor, or we're going to be late for our flight," Janeen prodded as Loralie looked for last-minute items to pack into the tiny spaces remaining in the aluminum case she wouldn't be letting out of her sight.

"You're like a kindergartner waiting to go on a picnic," Loralie teased. "Our flight doesn't leave for two hours. We'll get there in plenty of time to check in early."

"I guess I am eager. A watched pot never boils, and a watched clock's hands don't seem to move, either."

"I fail to see what all the excitement's about," Loralie teased. "You just talked to Jon last night."

"Liar," Janeen sniffed, wrinkling her nose. The expression on the interior decorator's face seemed to convey that she knew Loralie was every bit as eager to arrive in Indianapolis as she was.

"We'll be out of here in five minutes—or less."

Loralie was ready to head out the door when Jaydee came in. "You still here? I thought you'd be gone by now," he said.

"You and Janeen. She's been relentlessly nagging me about missing the flight."

"Traffic wasn't bad. You'll make it easy. If you leave now," he said.

"I'm going."

"Have a good trip."

Loralie started to go out the door, then stopped so abruptly that Janeen collided with her as she turned back.

"By the way, Jaydee, I accidentally opened a letter meant for you. It was mixed in with my mail. I slit it open and started to read it, then I saw it was addressed to you. Someone accidentally keyed in my 'Dept. L' on the envelope instead of 'Dept. JD'. I don't know how they happened to make such a silly error, although I suppose they could've seen both our ads and assumed I was using a 'key' to differentiate between ads in various publications."

"Oh."

"I didn't read it—or fill your order," Loralie teased. "It's on my desk. You won't have any trouble finding it."

"Oh. Okay. Good luck at the show—and goodbye."

"He seems eager to have you leave," Janeen said when they stepped outside.

"Not really," Loralie defended. "He's kind of a loner. I'm used to it now. That's just how he is."

The trip to the airport was uneventful, the flight pleasant, and they landed at the Indianapolis International Airport right on schedule.

"Time trials for the big Memorial Day weekend Indy 500 are going on," Loralie said. "No doubt the city is a hive of activity." Indianapolis was quite different from Atlanta and also from St. Louis. Strategically located, and the largest metropolitan area in the midwestern state, it was a hub for rail line, highway travel, and airline connections.

The women collected their luggage and took a cab to the downtown area, alighting at the same hotel where Jon and Denis would be staying, within easy walking distance of the Convention and Exposition Center—the Hoosier Dome—which was massive, although not as large as the Cervantes Center.

"Look! There's Union Station!" Janeen said.

"There's a lot to see here. I picked up a brochure and here is 'Circle', a Civil War Memorial—Union, probably. And also the World War Museum Plaza."

"I'll pass on a Civil War monument. I see quite enough of them at home," Janeen joked.

"I know. You'd rather feast your eyes on your Yankee boyfriend, right?"

"My, Miss Loralie, how intuitive you are today," she replied in a saucy drawl.

Loralie produced the brochure. "Indy's also home to the American Legion. That's neat. My father subscribed to their magazine for years and years."

"Mine, too," Janeen said.

"Oh! You might be interested in this. There's the John Herron Museum. It says it has a small, but excellent, collection and is a very good art school."

"Might be worth checking into if I get the time."

"We probably won't," Loralie admitted. "We'll likely end up spending our time at the Dome. Of course we'll go out at night. Jon and Denis have frequented Indy in the past when they've come to the annual shows here. I'm sure they'll introduce us to some great dining establishments. And maybe we can take a cab out to see the Brickyard where the race will be held."

"I don't care where I am. . .as long as I'm with Jon."

"I wish I felt as content and confident about Denis."

"You will," Loralie kindly assured. "You will. . . ."

Loralie had felt a sense of uncertainty. But once she and Janeen had checked in, freshened up, and then gone to the lobby to meet the men, the reservations melted away like snow in the face of warm spring breezes.

The night was wonderful. The food was excellent, the company charming, and the conversation was stimulating, as they never seemed to be at a loss for things to say. Finally Jon, Denis, and Loralie realized they were going to have to return to the Dome to unpack their wares which they'd deposited at the Convention and Exposition Center before they'd gone out for the evening.

"Gary Stanley is coming in this weekend," Loralie told Jon. "I got a card from him."

"Great. Maybe he can go out to dinner with us one night."

"That's what I'd thought. I'm sure that Denis will agree, too. And I do want Janeen to meet him. I'm sure she'll take to table-sitting as quickly as Gary did!"

Janeen got her first experience at that duty the next morning. "Nothing to it!" she said two hours later. "This is fun."

"I knew you'd enjoy it. Of course this show has some, ahem, 'built-in attractions' for both of us."

"Actually," Janeen said in a thoughtful tone, "I could really become accustomed to, and enjoy, this lifestyle. Jet-setting around, staying at quality hotels, chatting with people, having a good time. And you guys call this 'work'?"

"Jon might be very happy to hear such sentiments on your lips, my dear."

Loralie was away from the table browsing through other dealers' wares when Gary arrived from Edwardsville, Illinois. He'd introduced himself to Janeen, had taken the spare chair that Loralie had vacated, and the two were chatting like old friends.

"I see that you've met," Loralie said upon her return.

"We sure have. Now *this guy*," Janeen said, her tone meaningful, "*I like*."

"Thanks," Gary said. "That's nice to know. But something tells me that this is an inside comment."

"It is. Janeen's not too wild about my associate back in Atlanta."

"Soon to be her ex-associate," Janeen said. "And I don't think it'll be any too soon. He's graduating from Georgia Tech and moving on."

"I'll be graduating soon, too. I haven't really decided what I'll do. I made it into the National Honor Society for nurses. I know that I could get full-time work at some of the St. Louis area hospitals where I did my clinicals, but I may head for greener pastures, too. One thing about nursing, you can get work almost anywhere you go. So many states have reciprocity. I'm going to take the State Boards for both

Illinois and Missouri, although I may end up else-where. I'm serious about coin-dealing," he admitted. "I got to thinking that if I did private duty nursing, I could arrange my schedule so I could do both."

"Come to Atlanta, and I'll put you to work."

"Do you mean it?"

"Show up at my shop—and see."

"She'd be a real peach to work for," Janeen said.

"If you're serious, I'll consider it."

"Then definitely keep it in mind."

"In the forefront of your mind," Janeen stipulated.

"Now that that's settled, one more point of inquiry. Are you free tonight?" Loralie inquired.

"As a matter of fact, yes," Gary admitted. "I haven't been here long enough to have made any plans."

"Then don't bother, we've made them for you. Jon, Janeen, Denis, and I would like you to spend the evening with us."

"Maybe we can consider it a pre-graduation party!" Janeen suggested.

Although Loralie and Janeen were tired from the long day on their feet at the show, by the time they'd returned to their hotel, had showered and slipped into dressy outfits, applying fresh makeup, they both felt enthusiastic and ready to enjoy an invigorating night out.

"Don't they look handsome?!" Janeen whispered when the elevator doors hushed open and they saw the three guys waiting in the lobby.

"They certainly do," Loralie answered.

She was happy for her friend when she saw the

worshipful gaze Jon gave Janeen. But she felt even more elated on her own behalf when she discerned the tender look in Denis St. John's riveting brown gaze. And she was still more content when, before they partook of the food the waiter set before them, like the others gathered there, Denis St. John took a moment to bow his head and thank the Lord for the bounteous food He had provided.

At that moment, Loralie knew a wonderful sensation of true hope for a future with two hearts as one.

And when Denis swept her into his arms as they were sheltered behind a large, potted tree in the lobby, shielded from the eyes of casual passersby, the perfection of his kiss and his towering form over hers, thrilled her heart anew.

That night she went to sleep thinking about Denis St. John. And she woke up with sweet daydreams filling her every thought.

seventeen

The second day of the show was even more successful than the first. Gary Stanley exchanged fond farewells with his dealer friends, but only after Loralie had made clear a job was waiting for him in the Atlanta area. He promised to at least come down and check it out.

The foursome had plans to go out that night, but when the two women went to the lobby, only Jon was waiting for them. "I just got a call from Denny," he said. "He'll be detained. Something to do with ANACS business. We can go ahead and he'll catch up later."

Loralie, knowing how much Janeen would like to be alone with Jon, made excuses. "I'll wait for him."

"It could be hours, Lor," Jon said. "He sounded pretty uptight when I talked to him. He had a real edge to his voice, and his attitude was almost like what you endured in St. Louis."

"Oh. . .no. . . ." Loralie's heart sank. "Well. . .I'll wait. . .and if it gets too late, I'll order room service. Now scram, you two! Go out and have a good time. I'll be fine."

Two hours later, the telephone in Loralie's suite shrilled. It was Denny. "You're in," he said. "Good! Because I'm coming right up!"

Before Loralie could say a word, he'd hung up.

When she went to unlock the door for him, she heard the hum of the elevator already ascending, so she stood waiting in the doorway. As soon as he stepped through the elevator doors, she could see he was rigid with fury. He strode down the hall, bearing down on her like a runaway freight train, and Loralie felt raw fear at the look in his eyes.

"You-you-you—!" Words seemed to fail him. His sparking brown eyes said plenty, though. "You disgust me," he hissed at last.

"What are you talking about?" Loralie felt as though she'd been struck.

"Don't act so innocent," he sneered.

"Denis, please. I have no idea what you're talking about."

"I'll bet you don't, you lying cheat."

Loralie's own anger suddenly escalated. She clenched the fabric of her dress to keep herself from slapping his face.

"This is what I'm talking about," he raged as he pushed his way into her room. From the inside of his suit coat, he produced smeary, poor quality photocopies. The copies were clear enough to tell an ugly story. Especially when Denis threw a handful of coins onto the coffee table. The coins fell to the carpet, propelled by his red hot anger.

"I-I promise you—I don't understand." She grabbed the Gideon Bible from the drawer. "I'm telling you . . .that this is some horrible mistake."

"Save your professions of faith for the judge. Maybe he'll have leniency on you if you're sufficiently pious—and smile pretty enough."

"That's a cruel and undeserved remark."

"Pretty clever trick." Denis' tone was low and cutting. "You thought you were so smart. You must have figured that people wouldn't be observant enough, or bright enough, to put two and two together and come up with the right answer."

"I don't understand what this is all about."

"Sure you do!" Denis goaded. "You bought 1914 Lincoln cents with no mintmark from subscribers to some small publications. And then in other publications, you offered 1914-D Lincoln cents—altered coins, key date coins every collector wants in their collection. Your buy-sell trick was clever, but it wasn't good enough."

"I didn't do that!"

"A dealer friend of mine happened to notice that the same person who was buying the plain 14s was selling 14-Ds. So he ordered some and had some friends order a couple too. All fakes, just as he'd expected. To make the case more airtight, he specified they be shipped to him via the United States Postal Service. By the time the Postal Inspectors get through with you, Ms. Morgan, you won't be smiling over your ill-gotten gains. To think it was *you* behind the many 1914-D fakes suddenly showing up at ANACS headquarters."

"Oh, my goodness," Loralie whispered, clutching a chair back for support. "I didn't do it—but I know who did—"

"Of course you do! Your boy genius from Georgia

Tech. You probably hired him for a song—and made out like a bandit—laughing all the way to the bank."

"He's obviously been the one behind this—but it's not like it looks, Denis. Please, listen to me—I can explain."

"I've heard enough," he raged. "I was starting to trust you. But you're just like all women. Lying. Clever. Conniving. Hypocritical. You were so unendingly *Christian*—the better to hoodwink everyone. I may see you in jail before this is over— which is exactly where the likes of you belong!"

With that, he strode from her room, slamming the door behind him. The echo of the slam rang in Loralie's ears as she stared blankly at the closed door. Then her eyes filled with tears and she began to sob.

She was still crying when Janeen returned.

"Heavens, Loralie, what's wrong?"

In a voice choked with tears, Loralie explained.

"That rotten Jaydee!" Janeen gasped. "He's behind this! I know he is—"

"I know that, and you know that—but Denis believes I'm a fraud. That I'm a hypocrite, pretending ethics, while I actually have the heart of a shyster. That I hid behind a Christian, do-gooder facade."

"I'm going to call Jon. He'll know what to do. He knows you'd never do anything dishonest."

Minutes later the Boston coin dealer arrived. "So that's what Jaydee was doing with the 1914 Lincoln cents. No wonder he was so reluctant to let me see them that night we met."

"That's right! I'd forgotten about that," Loralie

gasped. "And this explains why he was so intent that I let him pick up the mail. In case the situation went sour, he could hide behind my name, and I'd get blamed for counterfeit material. He didn't want to use his own name, so he used the address key I used to keep my mail separate from his."

"He's a pretty slick character. Too bad he didn't keep his intelligence focused on more legal and beneficial undertakings."

"What are we going to do?" Janeen asked.

"We're going to cooperate. And we're going to help Denis build his case—a case against the guilty party—Jaydee. I'll be glad to testify that in my presence Jaydee had a roll of 1914 Lincoln cents with no mintmarks. That he said they had arrived in the mail that very day."

"Denis threatened me with the Postal Inspectors."

"He's right about the seriousness of anything that involves the Postal Service. But he's wrong to view you as the suspect. Calm down, Loralie, and let me handle this—and Denis St. John."

Loralie felt better with Jon in control. She sank to a sofa in the sitting room of the suite while Jon placed a call to Boston. From Jon's side of the conversation, she realized he was talking to a relative who was a small town postmaster.

"Okay, that's what we'll do. Thanks for the information."

"What did he say, Jon?" Janeen asked.

"He said we should put a hold on the mail to your box number, Loralie. Who rented it?"

"I did."

"You're sure? You didn't give Jaydee half the fee and let him do the paperwork?"

"No. I had the box number for a year or two before he and I even met."

"Great. That makes it a lot easier." Jon smiled reassuringly at Loralie. "What you need to do next is call the post office in Atlanta, and tell them you want the mail to your box number held. Talk to the Supervisor of Postal Operations, or the night supervisor. Someone high level. That way Jaydee can't get the delivery. With it as evidence, we can nail him dead. He won't get away with this. And he won't bring you down with him."

"What about Denis?" Loralie's voice was weak.

"Let's leave him alone with the Lord for a while. Maybe when he realizes what he's done, he'll feel bad. And when I go to his room in a little while—and tell him what really happened—he may even be convicted enough to experience a full-fledged conversion."

"If that could happen. . .then all this would be worth it. More than anything I want the eternal happiness of the man I really do love."

"He really loves you too," Jon assured.

eighteen

After Jon left, the wait seemed interminable. Loralie and Janeen had no idea what was going on in the room three floors beneath them.

When the telephone shrilled, Janeen rushed to answer. "For you," she said, gesturing to Loralie.

With trembling fingers Loralie accepted the receiver, brushing another tear from her reddened eyes.

"Loralie? Could you come to Denis' room? It's really important."

"Jon. . .I really don't know. I feel awful. I look awful. Can't this wait until morning?"

". . .He really needs you, Lor. Please come now."

"Here," Janeen said. "Wipe your face with this cool washcloth." She got Loralie's brush from the dresser. "I'll give your hair a lick and a promise, then you can go."

"I have to wait for Jon. He told me he'd come up and escort me to Denis' room so that I'm not walking the hotel corridors alone late at night."

"That's my Jon," Janeen sighed. "So thoughtful and considerate and protective."

The tender words were like a razor cutting across Loralie's heart. Because the man she'd come to love seemed to have none of those traits. But then, Jon obviously loved Janeen. And when Loralie remembered the scalding words on Denis' tongue, and the scathing look in his eyes, she died inwardly. She believed the man she loved despised the very ground she stood on.

"Don't worry, sweetheart," Jon reassured Loralie when he led her from her room and they proceeded toward Denis' quarters. "You can face it. You're not alone. The Lord will give you the words of wisdom you require."

Loralie didn't know what to expect. The Denis St. John who'd stormed from her room had been a man who seemed almost mad with his own power and authority. He'd believed he had all the facts, and that there was no need to look further—to trust further—to find the real truth.

The man she confronted now, however, was hollow-eyed, his face ashen, his features strained. He and Loralie stared at one another. Her lower lip trembled. Denis looked away, unwilling—unable—to meet her gentle eyes.

"I've learned what a mistake it is to be unwilling to trust enough to listen," he said, his voice hoarse.

Loralie gave a wan smile. "And I'm realizing that perhaps I have been entirely too trusting...." She was thinking how her own agreeableness had set her up to be used for another's deceptive plan.

"You must hate me," he murmured low. "But I can assure you, less than I despise myself. If I could but buy back the horrible things I said to you, Loralie, I'd liquidate all of my holdings to meet the cost. I realize, thanks to what Jon's said to me, that the Lord has forgiven me. But He's God. You're only human. I'm not sure that after what I've said, there's a future in which you'd take the time required to even think about forgiving me."

"You're right, Denis. I can't see any time in the future when I'd be forced to forgive what you said to me tonight."

"I was afraid it'd be like this," he whispered, and dropped his haggard face into his hands.

Loralie went to him and touched his shoulder. "I don't have to worry about forgiving you some time off in the future. Not when you're already forgiven, Denis. I forgave you as soon as you exited from my room. Long before you asked the Lord to forgive you. Now you must forgive yourself."

Denis stared at her as if he couldn't quite believe it. But from the look on her face, he realized it was true.

"Oh, Loralie. Loralie, my love. . . ." he whispered in a voice that held a deep timbre of emotion.

Wordlessly she opened her arms to him, and he stood up and moved into her loving, forgiving embrace.

"You're wonderful, Loralie. A true example of Christianity for me to strive for. A pearl of a woman. Everything I could ever want in the one I desire for mine."

"And you're the man I love and need, Denis, as we both adore and seek the Lord, and accept the blessings He has planned for us."

"I love you. But what mystifies me. . .is that you love me. You do—don't you?" he whispered.

"Very much so," Loralie murmured. "And with a fullness of emotion that tells me how true that love is, Denis. My love comes from God. . .for now that I know you are at last a man of God, I know ours is a love that's meant to be. It's a real and precious thing . . .always and forever. . . ."

A Letter To Our Readers

Dear Reader:

In order that we might better contribute to your reading enjoyment, we would appreciate your taking a few minutes to respond to the following questions. When completed, please return to the following:

Rebecca Germany, Editor
Heartsong Presents
P.O. Box 719
Uhrichsville, Ohio 44683

1. Did you enjoy reading *A Real and Precious Thing*?
   ☐ Very much. I would like to see more books
      by this author!
   ☐ Moderately
      I would have enjoyed it more if _____

   _____

2. Are you a member of *Heartsong Presents*? Yes No
   If no, where did you purchase this book? _____

   _____

3. What influenced your decision to purchase
   this book? (Circle those that apply.)

Cover	Back cover copy
Title	Friends
Publicity	Other _____

4. On a scale from 1 (poor) to 10 (superior), please rate the following elements.

    ___Heroine   ___Plot

    ___Hero   ___Inspirational theme

    ___Setting   ___Secondary characters

5. What settings would you like to see covered in *Heartsong Presents* books?

_____

_____

6. What are some inspirational themes you would like to see treated in future books?_____

_____

_____

7. Would you be interested in reading other *Heartsong Presents* titles?   Yes   No

8. Please circle your age range:

Under 18	18-24	25-34
35-45	46-55	Over 55

9. How many hours per week do you read? _____

Name _____

Occupation _____

Address _____

City _____ State _____ Zip _____

........Presents........

Great Inspirational Romance at a Great Price!

Heartsong Presents books are inspirational romances in contemporary and historical settings, designed to give you an enjoyable, spirit-lifting reading experience. You can choose from 60 wonderfully written titles from some of today's best authors like Lauraine Snelling, Brenda Bancroft, Sara Mitchell, and many others.

When ordering quantities less than twelve, above titles are $2.95 each.